October 31, 1985

October 31, 1985
Six Stories of Halloween

Joshua Coonrod

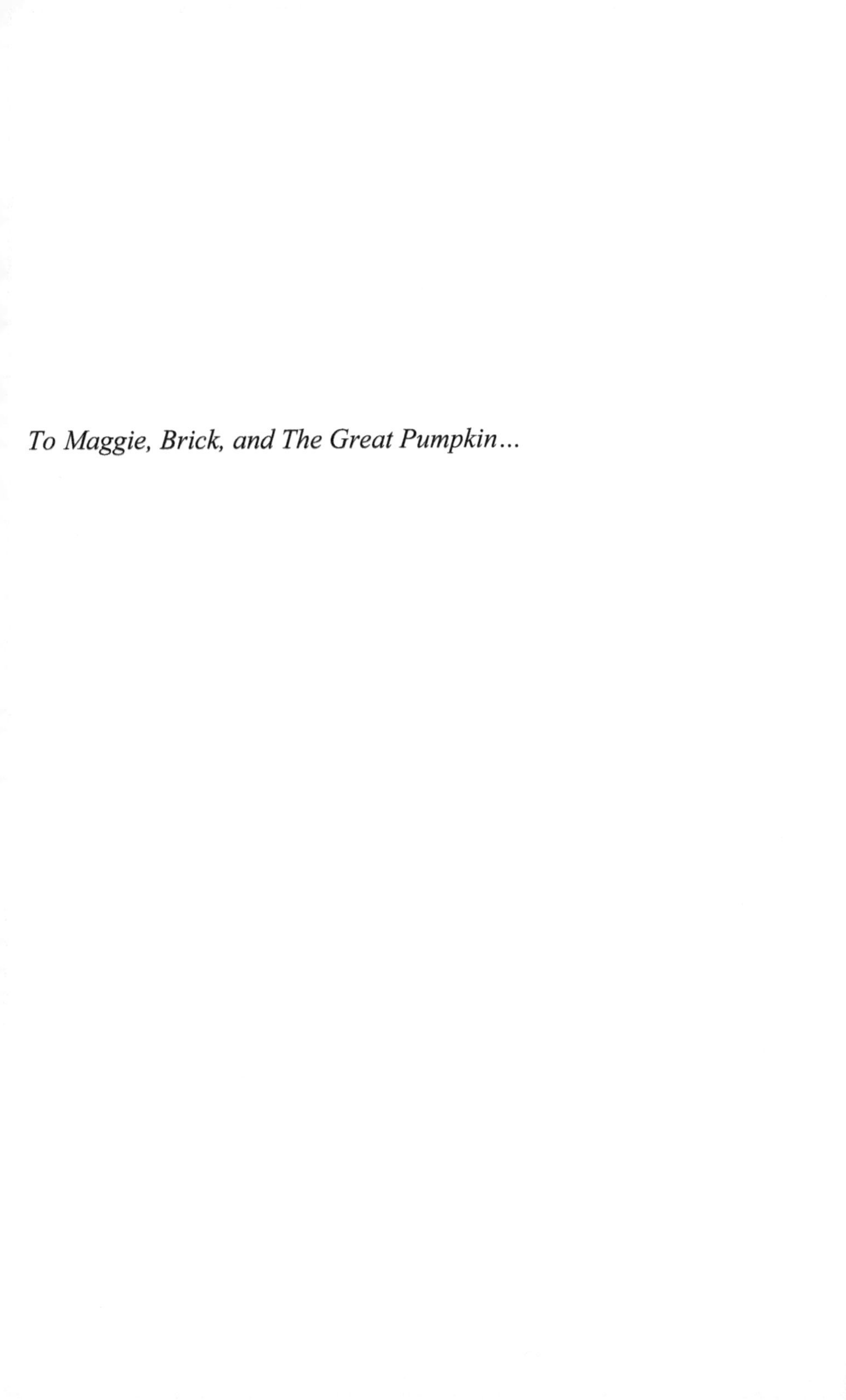

To Maggie, Brick, and The Great Pumpkin...

Contents

Forward

One thing the years have taught me is that there is no wrong way to celebrate Halloween. I've spent it trick-or-treating with my mom, partying with my friends, and staying in to watch scary movies with my fiancé and our dog. Some years it's more about the candy; some years it's more about the movies; some years it's more about the festivities. The only bad years were the ones that I told myself what I did wasn't enough - that I could have eaten more snacks, watched scarier films, or hung out with a few more friends. The best years weren't when I did the most. They were when I realized what I really wanted and dug into it - whether it was fashioning the most detailed Eric Draven costume from *The Crow*, making the journey up to St. Louis to hit the big-time haunted houses, or setting aside the time for a full *Nightmare on Elm Street* marathon. One just-right thing is always better than all of the-usual things in the world.

If you're reading this book in 2020, we're in the midst of some dark, scary times. The thing many of my friends have been saddest to lose is the celebration of Halloween. While the idea of missing out on a holiday might seem crass when so many people are sick and dying, it's still important to recognize and deal with the little things we're all losing right now. That might help you realize that while you can't attend a crowded holiday soiree or see the newest horror flick in a movie theater, you can try to assuage your sadness by focusing more on carving an intricate jack-o-lantern, driving through your local neighborhoods to check out the decorations, and finally making that list of horror movies you've been needing to watch for decades (make sure Michael Dougherty's *Trick 'r Treat* is on there if you haven't seen it yet.)

That's the spirit that led me to write this book. I've been wanting to put together a collection of Halloween stories for years, and this was the moment that offered me the opportunity to write them and prompted me to revel in the nostalgia of Halloweens past. Whatever your experience of the season is, I hope reading this might add a little orange-and-black flare to it. It was written to bring the memories of picking a costume, trick-or-treating, and eating candy in the 1980's to life in a way that makes you feel them. At the very least, I hope it can take you away from the real world for a few minutes (and at best, I hope it makes you pause before you switch off the lights at night.) Thank you more than I can articulate here for taking the time to read it. And no matter what day it is, Happy All Hallows' Eve - keep that spirit with you all through the year!

Sincerely,
Josh

October 31, 1985, Part 1

The Millers' television set was heavy enough to break a toe. Kevin knew this, because he'd seen it happen.

"Out of the way!" his father had shouted when they moved into their new house on Maple Street. Kevin's mom had hesitantly asked his dad if he should use the dolly to wheel the TV into the house. Kevin's dad chuckled and shook his head.

"The top of it is made to be carried, Heather," he'd said, pointing to the ornate wood that wrapped around the top of the thick glass screen. Kevin glanced up at the top of the TV, and he could see his dad's point. But he also remembered his dad saying that no one on Earth could guess how heavy that TV was just to look at it. Whatever mechanisms made images appear on the screen, Kevin was pretty sure there were at least three bowling balls involved.

The brief trip up the driveway to the front porch of the house was already shaky. What little existed of Kevin's dad's muscles bulged as he tried not to sit the television down once it was off the U-Haul. Kevin's mom darted around him, trying to hold open the front screen door while simultaneously squishing herself flat against the outside brick wall. Kevin's dad struggled to ease by, legs bowed for support, crab walking sideways, trying to suck in his stomach to get both himself and the TV through the front door. He made it, with Kevin running in just behind him.

"Kevin, be careful…" his mom shouted.

But had Kevin been any slower, he might have missed it. It was almost like one graceful movement - a cross between a ballet step and a car crash. Finally inside the living room proper, Kevin's dad stumbled forward so fast it looked like he would fall over. With Herculean strength, he managed to bring the television set up in the air so as not to trip over it...before dropping it directly onto his front right toe with an audible crunch.

What followed was a stream of obscenities unlike any Kevin had ever heard. He knew certain curse words could be combined, but he didn't know they could be linked and repeated constantly to form some kind of epic mutant vulgarity.

It would forever seem unfair that he wasn't allowed to cuss after that incident, but this didn't seem like the moment to bring it up.

The toe was mangled badly. Kevin's mom told him to cover his eyes when she sat his father down and peeled back the bloody sock to reveal a collage of broken toenail, bruised skin, and indistinguishable gore. But of course, Kevin peeked. If you never peeked, you never learned.

The rest of summer played out a little differently after that. Kevin's dad spent most of his time on the couch, toes bandaged together in open-ended shoes, grumpy that he wasn't playing softball and that he couldn't mind his new department store quite the way he wanted to. If Kevin didn't pay perfect attention to him, his dad would growl, "Don't make me be the one-legged man in a butt-kicking contest." He wasn't the same for months.

But give credit to Mitsubishi, the television itself was fine.

Today, Kevin was doing what he was usually doing - sitting a couple feet from the TV, legs crossed, staring deeply as the images from his favorite show played out in front of him.

He was a little frustrated. It was Halloween, and he felt like everything should be a Halloween episode on Halloween. But in the worlds of He-Man and the Silverhawks and the Incredible

Hulk, there never seemed to be any holidays. They went about their adventures, never stopping to celebrate their victories or enjoy the seasons. (To be fair to the Silverhawks, there didn't seem to be seasons in outer space.) Fair enough for them, but on October 31st, Kevin wanted everything to be orange and black and haunted by witches, black cats, and werewolves. It just felt wrong for his after-school viewing today to be yet another interplanetary space fight for John Blackstar.

He knew more Halloween specials should be on later, though. Some had already run the night before - *Garfield, Peanuts, Disney Halloween*. Actually, the more he thought about it, he didn't know what would be on tonight. He gazed into the rounded glass screen of the TV, pondering which shows he wasn't thinking of - and what he might miss while he was out trick-or-treating. That was always the complicated thing about holidays. He found himself wondering if they should put the best holiday TV on when people were supposed to be out celebrating the actual holiday. Which one was more important - watching Halloween shows or going house-to-house? The answer seemed like it should be obvious - Kevin loved candy - but he hated the thought of missing a single second of the best Halloween episodes.

"Kevin, you're too close to the TV!!"

His mom's voice punctured the haze of his thoughts. His eyes fluttered, and he looked around the room.

"No, I'm not..." he started to say, suddenly realizing he was sitting far closer to the TV than he meant to, only a couple feet away from the screen.

"We've talked about this before. Six feet away, or the TV goes away!" his mom said, half acting stern and half too amused by her own rhyme to keep up the act.

But she would do it. Kevin knew this, because she had done it before. He was constantly getting too close to the TV, and his mom couldn't stand it. She didn't like watching TV as much as

Kevin and his dad, and she got particularly mad when she thought Kevin was paying more attention to it than whatever she was telling him.

"Why don't you go outside?" she asked. "It's a beautiful day. Go play pretend!"

Kevin usually loved to play pretend, but he suddenly found himself a little foggy. The room had gotten a little darker than he'd realized, the sun setting a couple notches since he got home from school. He couldn't even quite remember when he'd sat down or who the Silverhawks had been fighting by the end of the show.

Pulling on his light jacket, the one covered in patches of baseball teams he didn't even know, he yanked the front door open and stepped outside. The cool air blew his hair around, waking him up a bit. He buttoned up his jacket, walked over to his favorite tree, and started to think about the weird thing that had happened in school today.

The Gargoyle

The new kid was hideous, but that was to be expected.

Everyone was suited up for the annual Fawcett Elementary School costume contest. Each year on Halloween, kids were encouraged to wear their Halloween costumes to school, and at lunch, they did a big parade through the playground for all the teachers and parents. Then that afternoon, they went into the gymnasium, and each kid walked in front of the whole school, and everyone cheered for them. There was even a prize for whoever got the biggest applause.

Kevin was starting to regret his costume, though.

He'd fought hard for a Ghostbusters costume from TG&Y. It had a plastic mask that looked like Peter Venkman, his favorite character from the movie, with a white rubber band that held it onto his head. It came with a plastic shirt that read "GHOSTBUSTERS" and had all the characters from the movie on the chest, and a pair of plastic pants that looked like the ones from the movie. His mom sighed when Kevin started begging for it, telling him she could make a costume that actually looked like what the Ghostbusters wore in the movie. But he wanted people to know exactly who he was, and this costume said it right on the shirt!

But staring at all the other kids, Kevin realized his costume didn't seem all that special. In fact, he'd already seen two other kids wearing it, and one was a smelly kid named Daniel that Kevin couldn't stand because he was always farting in class. Why would Daniel like the Ghostbusters? He wasn't cool enough to like them!

On top of that, the little rubber band that held Kevin's mask to his face kept pinching the skin around his ears and pulling his hair. The mask itself was uncomfortable to talk in. He kept lifting it up, which seemed to defeat the point of the costume, and the little rubber band was rubbing his skin raw in the process. Plus, he'd torn one of his sleeves by walking too close to the pencil sharpener in class. The real Venkman would be ashamed.

A lot of the other kids' costumes were cooler. One girl was the Stay Puft Marshmallow Man; Kevin wasn't sure why anyone would want to go as the bad guy, but she looked just like Stay Puft! She had the big bulging arms and legs, the funny little hat, and she even painted her face white. Sure, she was having trouble sitting in her desk with all of that padding, but it seemed worth it to actually look like the character you were going as.

There were witches, werewolves, vampires, ball players, princesses, even a Slimer that all looked so much more like what they were supposed to be than Kevin did. People kept complimenting each other on their costumes, but no one said anything to him. He felt like a dolt.

There was at least one kid that kept paying attention to him, though. And that was the new kid.

Kevin wasn't sure which class the new kid was in, or if he was even a new kid at all. But his costume was so good that no one could tell who he was during the playground parade or the costume party in the gym. He was dressed in all grey, even painted on his hands, and you couldn't tell where his mask ended. His costume looked like pieces of carved stone, like it was sharp enough around the edges that you could cut your fingers on them. The face was horrifying - a long, narrow, distended jaw jutting out from the bottom, bulging eyes and curved horns sitting above it, and a pitch-black mouth between the two that the kid must have been able to see out of. It was the scariest costume Kevin had ever seen another little kid wear, and he was surprised none of the teachers had taken him aside and called his parents yet.

It was when they were marching in the parade outside that the new kid first seemed to notice Kevin. Kevin was looking back and forth at the parents that lined the playground, trying to find his own. The eye holes in his plastic mask were cut so small he could barely see out of them, though, especially the people that were standing further off to the sides. He lifted his mask, revealing his real face, and that was when he noticed the new kid turn swiftly to look at him. Kevin thought it must be someone he knew just now recognizing him - but who? He knew what all of his friends were going as for Halloween.

Kevin's eyes drifted around the playground, looking amongst all the grown-ups for his mom or dad. He saw a lot of parents in overcoats, snapping pictures and pointing at the other kids - but no sign of his own. He didn't figure his dad could get away from work, but he thought at least his mom could make it. Maybe she'd lost track of time watching *Days of Our Lives*.

When he turned to look back at the line of kids getting ready to round the swing set at the far end of the playground, though, that's when he saw that the new kid was still staring at him - walking perfectly in sync with the others, his head twisting slowly to keep a perfect line of sight on Kevin. Kevin stepped to the side, slowed a little a bit, and almost caused a pile-up as Tommy Arthur bumped into him with his unwieldy Transformers costume.

"Hey!" Tommy shouted. "Keep going!"

"Sorry…" Kevin mumbled, still watching the new kid look back at him as the line rounded the large metal swing set. They were almost parallel with each other when Kevin finally decided to pull his mask down, suddenly aware that his costume should be situated as well as possible, just in case his mom was snapping a picture of him from somewhere he couldn't see. Out of the left eye hole, he saw the new kid's gaping bird mouth turn away from him just as Kevin's mask snapped back into place. He couldn't understand how the new kid could see out of that mask; the mouth didn't look like mesh. It looked as dark as any room Kevin had ever been in.

His spine wiggled back and forth as the new kid finished walking by him, one of those uncontrollable shivers that sometimes streaked down his back for no reason.

Kevin never saw his mom before the kids marched back into the gymnasium. He usually would have been a little disappointed, but he felt too distracted to worry about it.

As all the students sat on the hard gym floor, Kevin realized something. Which class was the new kid in? Just behind him in line had been Heather Adams as a fairy godmother - but she was in Kevin's class. And everyone from Kevin's class was there when the teacher took roll this morning. But right in front of the new kid had been Mrs. Stormes - and Kevin knew all the boys in her class. Was it a girl? Did girls ever dress like *that* for Halloween? But when he started to go through all the girls he knew in Mrs. Stormes' class, it seemed like they were all there, too.

Kevin scanned the gymnasium to find the new kid. He wasn't far away - two rows up and maybe a half dozen kids to the left. But he was sitting funny, kind of in between rows, in a spot to himself. It was like he wasn't sitting in Mrs. Stormes' class or Kevin's class with Mrs. Mellon.

And the kid's head was turned like he was staring right at Jenny Edgars.

Jenny wasn't wearing much of a costume - or at least Kevin thought it was a cop out. She was telling everyone she was Cindy Lauper - but she was just wearing a bunch of bracelets, pink tights, and glitter in her hair. It was pretty much what she looked like every day.

Kevin kind of wanted to tell the new kid he shouldn't stare at girls. Kevin's parents caught him looking at Lindsey Durber for too long at Arby's one time, and they teased him about it for weeks.

At the same time, Kevin didn't want to talk to the new kid at all.

The costume contest started, and Kevin turned his eyes toward the middle of the gym. Principal Bell was explaining how each kid should line up when their teacher told them to, then they should walk across the space in the middle of the floor. You were supposed to clap for the costumes you really liked (which Kevin hated, because it always ended up being people clapping for their friends instead.) The kindergartners started lining up.

Kevin wished he was standing next to a friend in line. He wanted to ask someone who the new kid was, but Tommy Arthur didn't like talking to anyone. The girl in front of Kevin - Allison Frewer - had made it perfectly clear that she didn't want to talk to Kevin ever, for any reason. He didn't know what he'd done to her, but he wondered if her stupid friend Kim had told her that he'd called Kim, well, stupid.

He sighed. Today wasn't as fun as it was supposed to be.

As Kevin's class lined up and crossed the gym, he tried to think about anything else. When it was his turn to show off his costume, he tried to stick out his chest and walk across the room with pride. But he ended up shuffling across the floor quickly when it didn't feel like many people were clapping for him. What really got to him, though, was how absolutely no one clapped for the new kid when he walked across the gym, his head twisting back and forth to look at everyone surrounding him. Usually at least a couple of your friends clapped for you. Did no one know this kid?

There was a small chip in the tile on the floor where Kevin sat back down. The gym floor was mainly white, speckled a little bit with black dots, and thin lines separating the tiles from wall to wall. He scratched at what looked like the grey rock under the tile where the chip was. It looked oddly like the new kid's costume. He really didn't feel like looking up at the new kid to compare, though.

A wave of chuckles went through the gym. Kevin lifted his head up to see what was the matter, but all he saw was a kid in a baseball uniform walking across the floor.

"What's so funny?" the girl next to Allison whispered to her.

"That's Michael Forrester, Judy's older brother. That's not a costume. He's a baseball player, and that's the only thing he ever wears."

"What a dork," Kevin said, looking over at the two girls.

They glanced at him, then looked back at each other and started giggling.

Kevin's head drooped back down toward the floor, but that's when he noticed the new kid again. His head had turned firmly toward Michael, twisting to follow him step by step across the room. He was almost standing up, with some of the other kids behind murmuring that he was blocking their view. The new kid said nothing, silently sliding back down into a seated position after Michael was done.

Principal Bell announced that a fourth grader named Todd had won the costume contest for going as a ninja. Everyone applauded, but Kevin didn't think it was fair. The Stay Puft Marshmallow costume was way more impressive. Todd just had more friends.

It was chaos as usual when all the kids stood up to go back to their classrooms. The last hour of the day was a Halloween party with their teacher, and everyone was always excited to get back and eat candy. Kevin had seen the bags of candy corn and suckers and Snickers on Mrs. Mellon's desk. He was shaking at the thought of cramming them into his mouth while he finally asked some of his friends about the new kid.

Wait. Where was the new kid? In the craziness of everyone leaving the gym, Kevin had forgotten about him. He looked all around him, at the front of his class' line and the back, but he didn't see him. It shouldn't have been hard to spot those huge curled horns, but they were nowhere to be found.

He kept an eye out all the way through the hallways back to their classroom, but there wasn't a sign of that creepy costume anywhere. It really started to bother Kevin, as if the new kid could appear right behind him at any moment. He didn't know what the kid would do, but when he thought about the deep, dark space in the mouth of his mask…

Kevin was brought back to reality by Mrs. Mellon, standing in the doorway of the classroom, handing an orange sucker with a white jack-o'-lantern face on it to everyone who walked through the door. Most of the kids had the wrapper off and the sucker in their mouth before they even sat down. There were shrieks of delight as everyone realized Mrs. Mellon had also put a Snickers bar on everyone's desk, along with a handful of candy corn on a paper towel.

It took less than a minute for the whole class to turn into a roar as all the kids started talking to one another, performing in their costumes, making fun of other students, and asking each other where they'd be trick-or-treating. Kevin went over to his two friends in class - Roger and Mark - and asked if they'd seen the kid in the grey monster costume with the curled horns.

"Yeah, that was dumb," Mark said.

"But do you know who it was?" Kevin stressed.

"Some stupid kid!" Roger retorted.

Mark and Roger laughed, but Kevin didn't think it was funny. He wanted to ask them more about it, but that's when Mrs. Mellon broke into everyone's conversations.

"Okay, okay, everybody, enjoy your candy. I wanted to tell you a fun story, though!"

The kids kept chattering excitedly, barely paying any attention to her.

"Does anyone know why we wear costumes on Halloween?"

"Because werewolves are cool!" shouted James Wright, who was dressed like a werewolf.

"That's not too far from the truth, James…" Mrs. Mellon said, but she trailed off as there was a knock on the door.

Before she could even reach for it, it creaked open. Principal Bell stuck his head into the classroom, looking concerned.

"Edna, can I talk to you outside real quick?" he asked.

Mrs. Mellon stepped through the doorway. The kids suddenly became quiet, a murmur taking over the class before it erupted into new conversations. Kevin looked back and forth at Roger and Mark, but they didn't look like they cared.

When Mrs. Mellon stepped back inside the classroom, she was just as distressed as Principal Bell.

"Class," she said, "have any of you seen Michael Forrester? He was the older boy dressed as a baseball player."

"No, he's a fourth grader!" James Wright shouted.

"I know James, but did anyone see him in the hallways when we were leaving the gymnasium? In the bathrooms or maybe sneaking out to the playground?"

The class was silent. Mrs. Mellon was trying to act like it wasn't a big deal, but all the kids could feel that something was going on. She turned toward Principal Bell at the doorway and put her hands up, mouth open, unsure what to say. Principal Bell shook his head and disappeared out of the classroom.

Mrs. Mellon never finished telling her story from earlier. Some of the other teachers poked their heads in the door, and once or twice, Mrs. Mellon stepped outside to talk to them. But she never said anything else to the kids. She let them play and eat their candy, smiling and nodding at various students from time to time.

Kevin thought about going up to her and asking about the new kid in the grey monster costume. He didn't want to stir up any more trouble, though. He sat and listened to Mark and Roger make jokes about how stupid everyone else's costumes were, but he didn't say much.

It was almost 3:00 when Principal Bell came back to their classroom, nodding with relief and giving Mrs. Mellon the okay sign. She let out a big breath and held her chest. None of the other kids seemed to notice, but Kevin was glad everything was okay. He took his mask off from on top of his head and set it gently on his backpack. He felt done with celebrating Halloween for the afternoon.

When the bell rang, only a few kids put on their jackets to leave class. The first group of kids that left to go home were the ones that rode the bus to homes far away from school. Then the kids who took the bus to neighborhoods closer to the school, then the kids who were picked up by their parents, and finally the kids who walked home. Kevin was in the first group, and there weren't very many of them.

The hallways were mainly empty as he left the classroom. The footsteps of a few other kids could be heard, but most of them must have been being picked up by their parents as a special Halloween treat. As Kevin took a left into the main hallway that led to the front door and the buses, he was surprised to find himself almost entirely alone.

And then, just before he got to the doorway out of the school, he passed by the big open door that led into the main office. That's where he saw Michael Forrester, in his baseball uniform, sitting in the chair outside of the principal's room.

Somehow, Michael was already staring at Kevin when he came around the corner.

Like he knew Kevin would be there.

It wasn't very far through that little hallway to the main doors leading outside. But with every step Kevin took, Michael's head twisted, always keeping in perfect alignment with Kevin. Michael's eyes didn't flinch. He didn't say anything. He barely even seemed to be breathing. But he was definitely watching Kevin the whole time.

Kevin gripped his mask. He suddenly wanted to put it on, but that seemed silly. If you put on your costume, just because an older boy looked at you, what kind of a wimp were you? How much would people make fun of you?

But when Kevin was almost directly in front of Michael, out of the corner of his eye, he swore he didn't see Michael. He saw those curling horns, those protruding eyes, that deep, hideous mouth. He could feel them.

Palms sweaty, he pulled his mask over his head. It was askew, drooping to the left, so he could just barely see out of the right eye hole, but it was on. He turned and stared back at Michael. It was definitely just Michael now. Staring at him. Directly.

Kevin was shaking as he looked back at Michael, looking him in the eye the best he could, but he didn't know why. And finally, Michael's head moved. He drifted to the side, looking at the kids walking up behind Kevin, the movement of his head slow and assured as ever.

Kevin couldn't feel his feet when he started moving again. He was surprised he didn't trip and fall over, his legs so shaky and numb. But he moved forward, almost propelled by the momentum of the other students.

He found his way up the steps of his bus. His driver, a big, jovial woman named Doris, shouted at him, "Hey, wait, who's under there?" Kevin lifted the plastic up just enough for her to make him out and let him by. He crawled up in the seat directly behind her and pulled the mask back down over his face.

He didn't take it off until he was home, sitting in front of the television.

October 31, 1985, Part 2

Kevin's favorite tree was an old oak tree in his family's yard with a ladder nailed to it. Well, not exactly a ladder, but a series of 2x4's that let him climb up to the thickest branch in the middle of the tree. There wasn't an actual tree house in it; the Millers didn't have enough money for that. But at least Kevin could play on a few of the sturdier branches.

Fall was his favorite time of year. When they first moved to this house in the summer, he would try to climb the tree in shorts, and the branches would scrape his legs and little bugs would crawl on his skin. He couldn't stay out too long, or he would get a sunburn. And it wouldn't be any fun climbing trees once winter rolled around. The 2x4's would ice over, and the snow would leak through his pants if he sat there too long. The freezing wind would burn his cheeks. And in the spring, Kevin didn't touch any plants at all because of his allergies. It was autumn, with its blue jeans and jackets and cool breezes and piles of leaves when he had the most fun.

For a minute, Kevin was happy his mom had told him to go outside. He sat on his favorite branch looking at the neighbor's Halloween decorations, then he hung upside down, and then he swung back and forth with his feet just far enough from the ground that he didn't have to worry if he fell.

But then he looked inside the big front window of their house, and he saw his mom standing in the middle of the room, just staring at the TV screen, not moving. He couldn't see what she was watching, but she was totally focused on it.

How was it fair that he couldn't watch TV but she could?! Adults were always doing stuff like that - telling you to do one thing while they did another. He wanted to stomp inside and tell her what he thought of that.

Just then, though, his dad came pulling up their gravel driveway in his pickup truck. Kevin dropped to the ground and ran toward the driver's side door. His dad popped it open, jumping down in slacks and a yellow work shirt, looking over a clipboard, scratching his dark moustache.

"HEY DAD!"

He almost threw his clipboard in the air, he was so shocked.

"Dang, bud. Don't sneak up on me like that."

"Why didn't you dress up for Halloween?"

His dad opened his eyes wide and shook his head a little. He could get overwhelmed with how often Kevin popped up from out of nowhere, a flood of questions right behind him.

"Well, adults don't dress up for Halloween."

"Some do! One of the teachers was wearing a witch's hat today!"

"Well, that might not have been a costume," he said, chuckling and nudging Kevin's arm. Kevin didn't get it. Did his dad think the teacher was really a witch?

"What's your mom doing in there?"

"She's watching TV!" Kevin told on her, turning to look at his mom, then turning to look back at his dad. His dad was now staring through the window, too, head tilted and looking confused.

"Huh...why's she standing like that?"

Before he could go inside and check on her, there was a loud crack in the distance. Kevin's head whipped around, and for reasons he couldn't understand, he wished he had his mask.

"Was that a gunshot…" his dad said, into the air as much as to Kevin.

Kevin started to walk to the edge of the yard, but his dad reached down and pulled him back.

"Hey, you hear a noise like that, you don't go toward it. You go *away* from it. Otherwise is a good way to get shot."

Kevin nodded, not sure why he'd headed that way to begin with.

"Might have been that kid down at the Jacobs house. You make sure you're staying away from him."

Kevin nodded again, and asked, "Are they bad people?"

His dad paused, trying to decide the wording he wanted to use.

"Some people just get into a lot of trouble for some reason, and they're one of those families. I'm not saying they're bad, but I just don't want you playing with their boy. Especially on Halloween. I bet he gets into a lot of trouble tonight."

"Why?"

"Teenagers get into a lot of trouble on Halloween."

"But he's not a teenager! He doesn't look that much older than the fourth graders."

"Well, kids like him get older faster. You stay away from him. I don't trust him."

Dirty Bones

Robbie Jacobs was accustomed to the whispers and stares his family was on the receiving end of.

He was having more trouble getting used to the idea that the ground had started whispering to him.

It had all begun a couple months ago. Walking from school to meet his mother at her job, voices appearing faintly from just under his shoes.

"Robbie...Robbieeee....."

The voices were quiet, but he knew they were there. What he didn't know was what they wanted.

At first.

Before that, he wondered what they could possibly want from him? His mom and him had nothing, except the house over their heads - and if the voices in the ground wanted that, he figured they could suck it straight into the dirt themselves.

But what did he have to give them? Worn out sneakers? A backpack with one strap broken and a hole in the bottom? Hair longer than he wanted it to be because his mom didn't want to pay a barber and he didn't trust her with a pair of scissors?

It had been over a year since Robbie's dad left. He didn't explain why, except to call Robbie's mom crazy, say he did everything around there, and act like they were lucky he was letting them keep the house. As they would find out, though, the house was nowhere near as close to paid off as he acted like it was.

Robbie's mom said his dad had probably spent all the family's money on "girls" instead.

Things went downhill quickly after that. Robbie's mom had always tried to keep up her appearance, keep a nice house, and keep Robbie out of trouble. Now, she didn't care about any of that. She didn't get out of bed for a long time. Robbie's grandma and aunt came in from out of town, but they didn't stay long. His mom told them she wasn't going anywhere, and that Robbie's dad might come back anytime. After a couple of months, she started getting jobs, but none of them stuck. She'd come home saying how much she hated everyone, how mean they were to her. And a few days later, she'd be looking for a job at another bank, then another salon, then another restaurant.

She'd always held tight to Robbie, though. Put her arm around his shoulders and told him that she'd never leave him. Sometimes she'd smell his hair, and sometimes she would cry.

That's when people started looking at them. When she dropped him off at school, when they went to the store, when he'd come by the places she was waiting tables. They didn't even try to hide it. Side glances, raised eyebrows. His mom would meet their stares, and then pat Robbie on the hands and tell him it was okay. But he wanted to be left alone, and that's the one thing no one would do anymore.

They were in the grocery store once, and his mom started sobbing in the bread aisle. One of the teachers from school came up from behind Robbie, grabbed him by the arm and said, "Here, maybe I can help you, son…"

Robbie hit him as hard as he could. He got expelled, and ever since, he was one of the bad kids - even though he just wanted everyone to be quiet and go away.

And that's when Rick showed up.

Robbie wasn't sure what Rick did for a living, but he worked at a bank, drove a Mercedes, and had the whitest teeth that

Robbie had ever seen. He also wore sunglasses everywhere, like it made him cool. Robbie thought it made him look like a schmuck.

Rick and Robbie's mom had met at Tito's, the Mexican restaurant where sometimes she waited tables and sometimes she tended bar. It seemed like a good fit for her because everyone was quiet and kept their heads down. No one stirred up Robbie's mom, and while she came home tired, she never came home mad.

But after she met Rick, Robbie never knew if she would come home at all.

"Hey, you're a big guy, you'll be alright, right?" Rick said one time when he picked Robbie and Robbie's mom up from Tito's, but only dropped Robbie off at their house. Robbie thought his mom would still be home that night. When he woke up in the morning, she wasn't there. He was pretty sure he was the only fifth grader who'd spent the night alone at home.

And that's when the ground started talking.

"Robbie...Robbie....."

He'd looked for the voices when he first heard them. Then he'd tried to answer them, even digging into the ground and shouting. Finally he'd ignored them.

None of the options changed anything.

"Robbie...Robbie..."

Like a slow, quiet scratching at the surface of the Earth, like something so close that wanted to get to him, that wanted to say something, but just couldn't quite. It went from being terrifying to annoying to a maddening pulse that seemed like it was always there, begging for something that Robbie couldn't give it.

He saw his mother start to change. She'd always cared about her appearance, other than when Robbie's dad had first left. But now she agonized over it, switching out dresses over and over for a single date, getting lost in the mirror for hours on her makeup, going through earrings, necklaces, and bracelets that she hadn't worn in years. And if the slightest thing went wrong - a spot on her shirt, a bad glance into the mirror - she all but broke down. She said she loved Rick, and she was so happy to be around him, but she seemed almost as miserable now as she was when Robbie's dad left. Nothing was ever good enough anymore.

But it wasn't all her fault. In the few months she'd been with Rick, Robbie saw him break dates with her countless times - half the time when she'd already spent an hour getting ready for him. Sometimes on the most important nights, when he'd promised her the nicest dinners at the fanciest restaurants.

Robbie's mom would usually spiral when that happened. She'd act friendly on the phone, but after that, Robbie never knew what was coming. She might quietly sulk back to her room, not to be seen for the rest of the night. She might start crying and shouting and throwing things. Sometimes her tone would turn mean, and she would swear Rick was with Michelle again, his ex-wife, and she'd curse Michelle for leading Rick along.

And then Rick introduced Alice.

Alice was Rick and Michelle's daughter from when they were married, just a couple years younger than Robbie. Rick had waited weeks into the relationship to say anything about her. But as soon as he did, he acted like Alice was one big part of their family - a part of the family he was more than happy to leave with Robbie and his mom at any time for any reason.

When Alice showed up, the voices from the ground got louder.

"ROBBIE....ROBBIE....ROBBIE..."

Robbie's mom acted like having Alice at their house was a good thing.

"You've got a little sister now!" she would exclaim, like she and Rick were already married.

Alice didn't feel like a little sister, though. She wasn't mean, but she wasn't much of anything. She was a quiet girl who spent most of her time around Robbie and his mom staring blankly around the house and waiting to leave. Almost anytime Robbie said anything to her, she shrugged. If he ever got a word out of her, it was usually a singular "yeah" or "no."

Robbie's mom encouraged him again and again to be nice to her, which left Robbie at a loss. He was trying to be nice to her. Why did people always assume he was mean? But no matter how hard he tried, she was unresponsive.

And Robbie thought he knew why. He'd noticed it one time when Rick had taken them all out to eat. Robbie sat across the table from his mom, Alice next to Robbie, and Rick next to Robbie's mom. Michelle had also been there on a date, and she stopped by the table where they were sitting.

Michelle was dazzling. Everyone there was looking at her, but not in the way that they looked at Robbie and his mom. She had on a tight, sparkly dress, but it wasn't too tight, and it wasn't too sparkly. Her silky white-blonde hair swept perfectly down either side of her face, and her skin was cleanly tan without a mark on it anywhere. And that's when Robbie looked over at Rick, and then to Alice. It was all so effortless. Rick and Michelle were just naturally perfect. He looked at his mom, with her fried blonde curls and heavy makeup, and he looked at the frayed strings dangling from the cuffs of his flannel shirt. He shrunk into the corner of the booth, just hoping no one would see him. When Michelle politely introduced herself to him and his mom, it just made things feel worse.

The voices from the ground got even louder and more persistent that night.

"ROBBIE....ROBBIE...ROBBIE...ROBBIE...ROBBIE...."

That was the one night he thought about telling his mom about the voices. But when they got home, she was quick to deliver bad news.

"Honey, Rick and I are going to a Halloween party this year. I'm going to have you take Alice around our neighborhood, and then Alice's mom is going to pick both of you up and take you around town."

Robbie was horrified. He loved Halloween, and even with him and his mom strapped for cash, he'd figure out a costume to trick-or-treat this year. He was going to wear his black jeans and his black sweatshirt, and he was even going to color the white parts of his shoes black. Then he was going to get into his mom's makeup and paint his face white. Then, whenever someone asked him if he was a mime, he would shrug and not say anything. It might not be the commando costume he wanted, but it would be good enough to get a few pieces of candy dropped in his pillowcase. Thank God they didn't have to do the stupid costume parade at the midde school that they made the elementary school kids do.

But now his costume felt worthless. His ingenious idea would look like junk to Alice and her mom. Why couldn't everyone just leave him alone?

"I don't want to do that…" he whimpered to his mom.

"Robbie, I don't ask you for much, but this night is important to me. And Alice and her mom are very nice people, and I'm sure you'll have a great time."

Funny, she hadn't called Alice's mom a very nice person the other night when Rick had cancelled their date just before he was supposed to pick her up.

And here it was - Halloween night.

The voices from the ground were louder than ever, their calls crowding over each other in disarray.

"ROROBBIROOROBBIEEEEROBBIE…..."

He tried to block them out as he pulled together his costume, rubbing his mother's makeup on his face, trying to make it white enough. What did they want? Why wouldn't they just leave him alone? Why did they keep getting worse?

He wanted to say something to his mom, but she was moving around the house at high velocity, trying to get her kitten costume to be just perfect. She had told Robbie to watch Alice, but Alice was fine. Rick had dropped her off there after school, all shiny and perfect in her fairy costume. Rick never even explained why Robbie and his mom needed to take care of her until Michelle could show up.

Robbie sat on the couch and put his hands over his ears, trying to feel better. He wanted his mom to calm down. He wanted Alice to go away. He wanted the voices from the ground to tell him what they wanted or to just be quiet.

He was almost crying when he looked up and saw Alice across the room. He understood. He got up from the couch and took her by the hand.

***

Angel, Robbie's mom, couldn't find her kitten ears. She was tearing the house apart, looking under pillows, between couch cushions, all around the kitchen table. They seemed to have vanished.

She needed to calm down. She knew it. She could tell she was stressing Robbie out, and the last thing she wanted was Alice going back to her mom - or God forbid, Rick - and telling them Angel was acting like a disorganized madwoman all night. This Halloween party was supposed to be perfect; everyone would see her and Rick there together, and it would make things so much more official. But it felt like everything was slipping right out of her grasp.

Why did everything have to be so hard?

When Marshall, Robbie's father, left them months ago, it felt like everything was over. She didn't know how to do anything. Marshall made good money at the electric company, and she was supposed to focus on raising Robbie. But Marshall couldn't keep himself under control. All the drinking. All the fights. Nothing was ever good enough, nothing was ever perfect. How could a slob like that be so mad that nothing was ever just right, her mother had asked her.

Her mom and her sister said she needed to sue for child support. But she wasn't sure where Marshall even went, and if she did sue, he would never come back. She couldn't even decide if she wanted him back.

She knew her mother thought she was weak. She knew her sister thought she should just get over it. But every morning when she knew she should get out of bed, it all felt pointless. Nothing was going to get better. There was no way out. There was nothing. She and Robbie would float through a life that was falling apart, and eventually she would die. That's all that was left at this point.

Even when she started working again, it was like she was being dragged through gears just to get through work each day. She would do it for Robbie's sake - counting other people's money, cleaning up other people's hair, bringing other people's food - but almost every moment of it ached. If she couldn't tell how hard everything seemed to be for Robbie, how sad he looked, how quiet he'd gotten, she would have just given up. All the miserable work for ungrateful people, it was all for him.

And then she met Rick.

He was at Tito's, drinking beers with friends, laughing a little too loud, but he seemed so comfortable. And he smiled at her, and he talked to her, and he waved for his friends to go ahead without him, and he kept talking to her. At a job where everyone was almost mute, Rick lit up the space with his jokes, his questions, his small touches to Angel's waist and arms.

She had introduced him to Robbie slowly, still unsure about how upset Robbie was with his father leaving. He hadn't lashed out at Rick, or even been unpleasant to him. Robbie was a good kid, despite what some people seemed to think, and he didn't cause trouble.

But she could also tell the whole thing must have disturbed him. He became even quieter, talking to her less, mentioning fewer friends from school, always staring down toward his feet. She could cheer him up and get him to talk from time to time, but it was never long before he was drawn back into his shell, avoiding everyone. She really wanted to help him more, but she didn't know how.

Rick was sucking up so much of her time. He loved her, but he asked a lot of her. He took her to nice places and introduced her to nice people, but he always wanted everything to be just in its place. Little comments about her clothes, her hair, her makeup...he looked so good all the time in his suits, and Angel wanted to keep up, but she just didn't know how he did it. It was as if how he looked when she saw him was who he was naturally, and she was a fraud, desperately trying to put on a face that wasn't hers.

When he started dropping Alice off at their house, she felt used at first. Did he think that she didn't have other things to worry about? But then she realized it made them that much closer to being a family. Alice getting to know Robbie, seeing him as a brother, getting used to their house, spending more time with them.

But why was Rick gone more and more?

Angel shook herself back to reality. Where were the kids? Robbie had been in and out of her bathroom as he played with her makeup, and Alice had been sitting on the couch. Turning a 360 in the living room, she realized they were nowhere to be found.

"Robbie? Alice?!" she shouted, her voice automatically rising with anxiety. It wasn't a big house, and there weren't many places for them to be.

"ALICE…." she shouted again, heading back to her bedroom, scanning the room, looking under her bed, ducking into the bathroom, and even pulling her shower curtain back.

Her heart began to pound harder than usual.

Had Robbie been acting even stranger today than usual?

"ROBBIE?! ALICE?!" she screamed, almost at the top of her lungs. She rushed into Robbie's room and threw open his closet. Nothing.

"ROBBIE AND ALICE, PLEASE ANSWER ME!"

She almost tripped running into the other bathroom, and she banged her knee into the door frame going back into the living room and then the kitchen.

Nothing.

She opened the door to the garage. Please don't let Alice be out here, she'll be a mess, Angel thought. And then she realized that it didn't matter if Alice was covered in dirt head to toe; she just wanted to find her.

She rushed out into the front yard, dewy overgrown grass brushing her ankles. It was empty. No kids were even milling through the streets yet for trick-or-treating.

But it seemed dark for no kids to even be out yet. Why was it so dark?

She ran around the corner of the house, heading to the backyard. She swore she could feel the ground shaking underneath her feet.

For a moment, the backyard looked empty, a small rectangle of grass leading back to the line of trees behind it. But it was just light enough to see Robbie in the distance. He was facing away from her, looking down at...something.

She rushed behind him - through the yard, between the trees - and found him staring down at a pile of dirt in the ground. A pile of dirt that almost looked large enough to hold a person.

"Robbie...Robbie, move...." she managed to say, dropping to her knees and starting to claw at the dirt in front of her.

"Mom...." Robbie said.

The soil was loose, and Angel's hands moved right through it, but they found nothing. For a second, she thought she saw a few strands of pale blonde hair like Alice's, but in a blink, they were gone.

"ROBBIE, HELP ME," she shouted, the loose ground scattered everywhere, now down to hard earth that her fingers couldn't penetrate.

There was something here. There just had to be. She could feel it. Why couldn't she find it? Why couldn't she see anything?

"Mom…" Robbie said, pulling on the back of her black cat costume.

She turned, eyes wide, tears running down her cheeks, face and hands covered in dirt. She looked wild and confused - but Robbie looked as calm as he had in months.

"They don't want us, mom," he said. "We're not good enough. They just want them."

October 31, 1985, Part 3

Kevin's mom was startled when Kevin and his dad came through the front door. She turned from the TV with a sudden jerk, almost like she'd been caught watching something that she wasn't supposed to. But it was just the news.

"You okay, hon?" Kevin's dad asked.

She looked dazed.

"It was just, a, um, news story on being careful tonight. Just a lot of...uh...a lot of characters doing a lot of stupid things out there," she said. "We're keeping an eye on you, kiddo."

Kevin shrugged. He didn't want to be treated like a baby, but he was honestly kind of glad they were going with him.

"We should probably go ahead and get him in his costume," Kevin's dad said. "It's already getting real dark out there. Earlier than I'd expected."

"Oh, you never notice anything when you're at the store all day," she responded.

"Yeah, yeah, yeah. I feel like we were out all night last year with everywhere we went. Better to just get a jump on it. I don't want him to be grumpy on the way to school tomorrow."

Stupid years when Halloween was on a school night, Kevin thought.

"Well, he should eat something before he goes. It's going to be cold tonight. Let me heat up some chili," his mom responded, turning to look at Kevin and say, "Mmmmh, chili."

Kevin hated chili, but his parents refused to accept this.

As they sat at the dinner table, eating quickly, Kevin kept feeling more and more scared about going out. He didn't know why; he'd been trick-or-treating for years, and his parents would be right there. But he felt a warmth radiating from the television in the other room. He wanted to stay next to it and put on whatever Halloween cartoon was on TV. It just felt safer.

But candy, Kevin thought. You have to get candy.

The squeak of his dad's chair as he pushed off from the table brought Kevin back to his senses. What was he thinking? Not going out for Halloween? That was crazy. Who would ever not want to go out for Halloween?

He went to his bedroom and put on a T-shirt and a long-sleeved shirt as well. His mom promised him that if he wore enough layers, he could pull his costume over it all and not have to wear a coat that would cover up everything. He was worried the tear in his sleeve from school might rip more in the process, but it slipped right over his shirts. He was good to go.

His dad was in a heavy jacket and jeans when Kevin came back out into the living room, plastic Halloween sack in hand. His mom was fumbling with the camera to take a picture of them before they left.

A cartoon played on the TV. Kevin hadn't seen it before, and he turned to figure out what it was. There was a cartoon mouse - or was it a squirrel? a chipmunk? - talking to a shaking skeleton with yellow eyes.

"But I don't want to stay in the creepy castle, Benny," the skeleton said in a cowardly voice, bony knees shaking.

"That might be the only way to save Halloween, though," the dashing rodent fired back in an enthusiastic voice.

"But I heard that the people that pass over the moat and under the castle's archway of terror and stay in the castle past midnight will *die. I don't want to die, Benny...*"

"Everyone dies, skeleton. You're already dead."

Kevin's eyes opened wide as a burst of static filled the screen. He shook his head, wondering if he heard what he thought he heard. But the two characters were gone when the picture came back. Instead, it was an image of a castle archway, with the camera pushing into the deep darkness that sat within its old stone arch.

"Ready to go, bud?" Kevin's dad asked as his mom snapped a bright picture with flash.

"Yeah..." Kevin said, walking toward the door while his mom took one more picture. His dad rustled his hair on the way out the door, but Kevin barely noticed. He was glancing back at the television.

The image on it was pitch black now.

Devil Boys

Charles Dunt was one of Kevin's best friends, but they didn't have classes together. They played with each other when they could, but Charles' parents didn't let him do night-overs yet. They wouldn't even let him go over to a friend's house unless they were there the whole time.

It made Charles feel lonely sometimes, so he was extra excited when he saw Kevin trick-or-treating with his dad downtown.

"Mom, there's Kevin!" he shouted pointing. He started to walk toward him, but his mom grabbed his arm and held him back.

"Be careful, Charles, there's people everywhere!"

He wasn't sure what she was so worried about. Most of Main Street had been closed off so that kids could run back and forth freely, getting candy from each of the individual shops that lined the road. Half of the kids didn't even seem to be with anyone at all - though Charles' mom assured him that most of their parents must be around somewhere.

Yeah, they just didn't feel the need to stand next to their children every single second of the day, Charles thought.

"He's just down there at the paint store! It's only two stores away!"

"Charles, don't get too wound up. We can go home if we have to."

He sighed. He thought this Halloween would be better than last year's. No one else's parents were treating them like a baby. But this year had already gone wrong in so many ways. Charles had wanted to be the Incredible Hulk for Halloween, but his mom said she didn't want him wearing green face paint and hairspray. A couple of days later, she came home with a cowboy costume she thought was cute. When he said he didn't want to wear it, she said he didn't have to go out at all. Then when they were getting ready to go out tonight, he started listing different friends' houses where they could trick-or-treat. His mom shut him down again.

"We're not going and bothering people in other neighborhoods. We'll go downtown, and we'll do our neighborhood where we know everyone - but that's it."

He'd moaned, but she shot him a sharp look that let him know the conversation was over.

Charles was so glad to see Kevin, but even as they walked over to him, his mom put herself between the two boys and started talking to Kevin's dad.

"Hi Roy, how are you all doing tonight?"

Charles snuck around her to talk to Kevin, hoping that she was too focused on whether or not Kevin's dad had been drinking to pay any attention to him.

"Hey, how are you doing so far?" Charles asked. Kevin looked down into his candy sack.

"Okay. I've got a lot of Smarties. But no one's giving out any Junior Mints. Those are my favorite."

Charles thought Kevin sounded a little off, like he wasn't paying attention or he was tired.

"Yeah, I've got a lot of Smarties too. And a lot of raisins."

Kevin nodded a sad understanding.

"Hey you two, what are you doing?!"

Boone, a loud little chunky kid from Charles' class, appeared next to them. He had a buzzcut and red cheeks from the cold, and he was wearing a St. Louis Cardinals football jersey.

"Just trick-or-treating…" Charles said, nervous. Boone was the exact kind of kid his mom didn't like, and he felt like he might get in trouble just for Boone coming up and talking to him.

"No one's giving out any chocolate around here! It's all Smarties and raisins! It's so stupid, I hate this place so much," Boone shouted, garnering a wary glance from Charles' mom. "Let's keep going. You can pretty much go in a circle here the whole time. They're not paying any attention to which kid is which."

"I don't think I'm allowed to…" Charles started.

"Mr. Miller!" Boone shouted. "Is it okay if we walk to a few stores and get some more candy?!"

Kevin's dad nodded.

"I think that'd be okay, as long as you don't go too far," he said. He looked at Charles' mom who didn't seem to share the sentiment. "That'd be alright, right, Julie?"

"I guess if you stay in eyesight…" Charles' mom began.

Boone had already grabbed Charles by the arm and started to pull him away from his mother's side.

"Sometimes you just have to know which parent to ask!" he whispered.

Boone guided them down the street toward the end of the block, and once there were enough people between the boys and their parents, he quickly turned the corner and headed down the street.

"Wait, where are you going?" Kevin asked.

"If you go to the movie theater, they're handing out entire boxes of candy!" Boone shouted.

"We can't walk all the way over there!" Kevin shouted.

"It's not that far! It's just down the block and you cut through the park, and that puts you at the back of their parking lot! We'll be back before they know it!"

A shiver went down Kevin's spine.

"I...I can't," he said.

"Don't be a baby!" Boone said, but Kevin was already walking back to Main Street.

Charles stood there for a second. He looked at Boone's eager face, and then he glanced back up toward the street where his mom was waiting.

"Kevin!" he yelled. Kevin turned back to wait, but then Charles yelled, "Don't tell my mom where we're going!" Kevin shook his head and kept walking.

Boone and Charles started walking down the empty street toward the train tracks. Charles could see a single light shining in the park a couple hundred yards away, and he told himself once they got to it, they would basically be at the theater.

"My mom said we're not allowed to go to the movie theater because I'm gonna get enough candy anyway," Boone said, already so hyper with sugar that he was slurring his words. "But I'm gonna get a whole thing of Whoppers and see how many I can put in my mouth at once!"

That sounded really unhealthy to Charles, but he shook the thought out of mind for sounding too much like his mother.

The space at the end of the block, past the train tracks, was dark, and as the two of them crept up to it, Charles held his breath. It didn't seem like anyone would be doing anything dangerous this close to where people were trick-or-treating, but the shadows made for a deep dark that could hide anything.

They were just past the train tracks when they heard it.

"Look...over there...those two..."

Kevin's head whipped to the side to see a few figures moving in the dark. They were coming toward them. Fast.

Boone made an incoherent, high-pitched noise and then stumbled back into Charles. The figures were flocking toward them quickly, and all Charles could think to do was take off into a sprint, cowboy hat flying off his head. He heard Boone start running behind him, both of them heading for the light in the middle of the park.

Running wasn't easy, though. Part of Charles' costume was a pair of cheap boots that were too big for him, and his ankles risked rolling to one side or the other with each step he took. He knew he couldn't make it much past the lights at the basketball court before whatever was behind him caught up.

He wasn't sure if Boone was still there.

His right boot hit a patch of loose soil before he made it to the concrete of the basketball court, and his foot slid out behind him. He went down hard on the court, bag coming loose from his hands, candy flying everywhere. He rolled over on his back to see what was coming after him.

A grotesque rotting face floated just above him.

It let out a guttural scream.

"UUUURRRRRRR!!!"

Charles screamed

"RRRRUUURRR!!!!!"

Charles couldn't breathe and tears were running down his face. He locked his eyes close, hoping this thing would think he was dead and not proceed to disembowel him.

"Wait, dude, stop, he's crying!"

It was...an adult's voice? Or at least a teenager? But no matter what, it was human.

Charles opened his eyes and looked around. The terrifying face that had stared down at him was now dangling from the hand of an older boy standing a few feet away. He was bigger, with camo pants and a crew cut. To the right of him was another older boy, skinnier, wearing a black shirt with a red upside-down star in a circle on it. Between them, Boone was shaking, eyes almost bulging out of his head.

"Sorry, kid, we didn't mean to scare you that much," the skinny one said.

Charles stood up, looking for his lasso and seeing where all of his candy had gone. It was everywhere.

"I wasn't scared," Charles lied.

The skinny kid started picking up candy from the basketball court.

"Dude, what are you doing?" his friend asked.

"Do you want them to tell their parents on us?"

The other friend shrugged and started picking up the rest of the pieces.

"Which way are you headed?" the skinny one asked.

"We're going to the movie theater to get free boxes of candy!" Boone shouted, no longer shaking, driven by his quest for candy once more.

"That's a long way, dude."

"No, the back of the theater is just over there!" Boone shouted, pointing forward. The older boys looked skeptical.

"We'll take you over there for one of your Milky Way's," the kid with the crew cut said.

"Deal!" Boone shouted. He started that way before they'd even finished picking up Charles' candy.

Charles started to worry as they walked further into the park. They were leaving behind the one light they had, and he wasn't sure how much he trusted two older boys that had just scared them to death for no reason. And the more he thought about it, he didn't trust that Boone knew where he was going, either. Was the movie theater that close?

He suddenly realized his mom must have noticed they were gone by now. What would Kevin say when they saw him? How much trouble was he going to get into?

No, he thought. I'm doing this. I'm already in trouble, so I might as well.

They continued through the darkness of the park.

"You sure this takes us to the theater?" the skinny kid asked. "It seems like it's way further that way."

"No, I measured it once," Boone said. Charles looked at him with his eyebrows up. That didn't make any sense.

"What were you guys doing out here?" Charles asked.

"Nothing," the skinny kid said.

"Why weren't you trick-or-treating?"

"Ha!" laughed the one with the crew cut, polishing off the end of Charles' Milky Way. "We're way too old for that."

Not too old to eat all my candy, Charles thought.

He was ready to give up. They were who knows how deep into the park, butting up against the woods, no movie theater in sight, a hyperactive Boone for their guide. If only he'd chosen to turn around and go back.

But then they saw the fire. They'd come up over a small hill, and the flame was close enough to surprise all four of them. It was a little past the tree line, next to a creek that ran in a ravine through the park.

"Whoa, what's that?" said the skinny kid.

There were three men gathered around the fire, one standing above it, directing his arms like he was conducting a marching band. He wore a dark robe.

"Awesome..." said the other older boy, and they started down toward the fire.

"Wait, guys, we're supposed to be getting candy..." Boone protested. They weren't paying attention, though. They were mesmerized, drifting toward the strange fire that seemed to be growing higher and higher.

"Come on, let's go," Boone said, but Charles wasn't sure they should turn their back on this group. And as one of the men looked up and started stalking toward them from the creek, he knew he was right.

"Where you boys going?"

The man was large, big arms jutting out of a flannel shirt with the sleeves cut off. One bicep had a huge tattoo of a goat's head, the other one sporting the skull of some hideous creature the boys had never seen. He bent down, and Charles could see sweat beading on the man's moustache.

"He told us you'd come," the man said. Charles wanted to get away, but he knew he'd never outrun an adult, especially in his loose cowboy boots.

"I don't know who you're talking about, sir, but we've got to get to the movie theater and get some candy," Boone said. The man reached out and took Boone by his arm before he could get away, though.

"No. Come meet my uncle instead. He's got someone he wants to introduce you to."

There was no way around him. The man stood up and walked behind the boys, his hands gently pushing them forward. Charles swallowed hard. He was trying not to start crying again.

Both the older boys were now seated by the fire, its glow lighting their blank stares. Across from them was someone who looked similar to the man leading the boys to the fire. He was a little smaller, without a moustache, and he stared at the boys like he wanted to eat them.

The man in the robe looked down at them. He didn't remove his hood.

"Hello, children. We've been waiting for you."

A few long strands of grey hair fell from the hood. Charles couldn't tell for sure, but it looked like his left eye might have been totally white.

The hooded man started to walk around the fire, with the slightest of limps. The gaze of the two teenagers and two other men never left him.

"I know you might feel confused right now, boys. But that is because you have been lied to," said the man in the hood. "Most everyone in this town has been lied to. We stand on some of the most sacred ground on this gateway that we call Earth.

"Can you hear it?" he asked. "If you listen closely, it will talk to you. It will tell you what it wants."

At first, Charles only heard the crackle of the fire. But then did he hear...voices?

"And if you give it what it wants, it will give you what you want. You may think I sound mad, but there is a reason I am here today. The ground beneath our feet told me to be. It told me to find you here. It told me the story of our humble town...."

He bent to look the boys in the face. His grizzled skin and white eye were clearer than ever. But he didn't smell bad, like Charles thought he might. He didn't smell like anything at all.

"Before there was anyone else here, there was one man. One, single man. And he didn't know how he had gotten here. He had always been here. He built a home, and he lived off the land. This place was his.

"But see, then came another man. And the new man told the old man that how he was living was wrong. He said that together, though, they could change all that. They could make this place where the old man lived perfect. They just had to work together. They could wrangle food, and build homes, and tell stories, and it would be a paradise on Earth. The old man just had to trust the new man, and all would be well.

"And when the new man extended his hand in peace, the old man cut it right off of his body.

"As soon as the new man's blood spilled to the ground, great trees, and cool streams, and fatty animals lept from it. And the more the new man bled, the more wonderful this paradise became. And the old man sat back and enjoyed this wonderful new world, for the old man knew that greatness lay not in trust but in strength."

The man drew a curved blade from the depths of his robe.

"You boys are lucky it no longer takes that much blood."

He looked from Boone to Charles and back to Boone.

"A test of the innocents," the man said. "Of innocence."

He reached forward and scratched Boone's cheek with the blade just hard enough to draw a drop of blood.

"Thank you, boy," the man said, and he turned to place the blade into the fire.

A tiny glow started, right where the flame first touched the metal. A pure, white light. The man let go of the blade, and it disappeared into the spreading illumination.

Charles started to quake as the white light took over the entirety of the flames. He couldn't tell if the world was shaking around him or if he was just starting to lose control of himself in fear. He watched as the two teenagers and the two men kneeled down in front of the flame, and the hooded man bowed down to it as well.

Charles wasn't sure what he expected to see. Maybe the devil himself. But what he saw instead looked more like a worm. A long, squirming, slimy piece of meat slid from where the light met where the ground should be. It twisted this way and that, almost like it was trying to figure out which way to go.

It kept coming, revealing itself to be longer and longer. Not even intending to, Charles stepped back away from the writhing worm, realizing it had hard spots in it that almost looked like knuckles in a finger, and it contorted at those points in particular. Flashes of movement above him made him realize that this wasn't the only worm; more of them were reaching up into the sky.

As more and more of the worms slid from light, the ones in the air climbed higher and higher, almost like thin little tentacles trying to touch the moon. But the ones on the ground braced themselves against the earth, pushing upwards. Then, in between the worms in the sky and the worms on the ground, it came into view. It almost looked like a cage of ribs, but made out of weathered stone, with an indistinct fleshy mass pulsing inside of it, each worm extending out of it.

For a moment, it was still, raised a dozen feet in the air, in all of its grotesque glory. The men were frozen, looking up at it, speechless.

Then a dark hole in the fleshy center opened up, and a large eye appeared inside it. The worms floating above it swooped downward.

The men had no chance to move as the worms entered into their eyes, and ears, and mouths. Their peaceful awe was broken. They struggled and tried to scream as the worms began to retract, drawing the men toward where the thing's eye had been for but a moment, once again an ever darkening hole inside its center.

Charles might have stayed there in shock, letting himself be dragged into the void, if he hadn't felt Boone brush past him, running away. Charles started running as well, as best as he could with his feet rocking from side to side in the oversized boots. And for a second, he thought this… this thing must not want the boys. Otherwise, it would have taken them when it took the men.

And that's when he felt the slimy flicker on the back of his neck.

He pushed hard, rushing toward the peak of the hill that they had come over minutes beforehand. He passed by Boone, barely giving him a second look. He felt the buzzing of those little worms on his arms, like a swarm of gnats gathered around him.

Boone screamed.

Charles didn't look back, though.

He heard Boone scream again, but it was cut off in a gross, wet gargle.

After that, Charles was over the hill. There was no sign of Boone. He went as fast as his legs would let him, not slowing down until he'd crossed the train tracks and almost made his way up to the empty block next to Main Street. People were still trick-or-treating like nothing had happened.

He turned in a circle. Boone was gone.

A police officer was standing at the corner where Charles, Boone, and Kevin had turned off the street. Charles ran up to him, unable to say anything.

"Hey! Are you that Charlie kid?!" the officer asked. Charles hadn't even been able to respond before the officer was radioing to someone on his walkie talkie. "Hey, I think I got that kid that lady was looking for over here. He's freaking out."

Charles never said anything to that police officer other than nodding and shaking his head. He couldn't get his throat to open up to respond. It was like he was crying, but no tears were coming out.

His mom was a mess when she got there. Her hair frazzled, her makeup running, she hugged Charles and shouted at him, and he could barely make out what any of it meant.

When the police officer was gone, and they were headed back home, Charles finally calmed down enough to try and tell his mom what happened. He didn't know what to say and what to leave out, though. She would never believe all of it. But...but wasn't something horrible happening? Didn't they need to stop it? Hadn't anyone else seen the thing that crawled out of the ground by now? *Where was it?*

He started to tell most of the story honestly, and when he got to the men down by the creek, his mom gasped.

"Satanists! That's what they said on the news! They're everywhere right now! Charles, you have to be careful…"

"But...but they didn't say anything about that, mom," he tried to explain.

"Oh, they're all the same. They're crazy. And you don't want to know what they'll do to a little boy like you! Did they hurt you?!"

"No, they… they just said this thing about the town and the ground, like it was haunted, and told me some story about an old man and a new man, and how the ground would give you what you wanted…" He trailed off, noticing the air had suddenly gotten very still in the car. His mom was completely silent for once.

When she spoke, she spoke very deliberately.

"Charles, you forget all about that for now."

"What?"

"You forget about everything they said. You're not old enough for that yet."

He didn't understand what she meant. But when he tried to ask her to explain, she just shot back, "Be quiet. You're not old enough. That's enough for now. *Enough.*"

Charles' breath caught in his throat.

He really hoped Boone would be in school tomorrow.

October 31, 1985, Part 4

Kevin was eager to leave downtown when they finally could. He'd already felt weird before he'd seen Charles and Boone. He got more worried when they'd left for the movie theater. And he was terrified watching Charles' mom break down when she couldn't find her son. His dad insisted on staying with her until her son turned up, but as soon as the cops radioed that they'd found him, she told Kevin and his dad to go ahead and leave. Kevin was glad to, but the damage had been done. Nothing was going to make this Halloween fun again.

On their way back home, though, his dad said, "I think there's time to go by one more spot. Want to do Walnut Parks? You always get good stuff there."

Kevin wanted to say no, but what kind of kid said no to more trick-or-treating? He wanted things to feel okay again. Maybe if he got enough candy to really pig out when they got home, he'd be able to relax while he watched some Halloween cartoons.

"Let's do it!" he shouted, feigning enthusiasm.

Walnut Parks was the fanciest neighborhood in town, where most of the people with the biggest houses lived. And unlike the nice neighborhoods outside of the city, the houses were pretty close to each other here. You could knock out a dozen big houses that would probably give you a good candy bar in fifteen minutes. The more he thought about it, the more excited he felt.

His dad pulled up to the small playground that sat at the edge of the neighborhood. A number of cars were already parked there, everyone knowing the best place in town to hit. As they pulled up, he saw a girl from just above his grade, Amber Allen, getting out of her mom's minivan. He liked Amber. She was one of the only girls that was ever nice to him.

"Hi Amber!" he shouted, waving frantically.

She smiled and waved back, but by the time he and his dad were out of the truck, she was gone, around the corner and into the depths of the neighborhood. He thought that maybe if they hurried, they could catch up to her.

"Slow down, bud," his dad said. "It's dark out here. You don't want to go running out in front of cars."

By the time they rounded the corner, it was too late. There was no sign of Amber. Maybe they'd catch up to her later.

As they started down the first of the neighborhood streets, Oak Avenue, Kevin was surprised to find barely a single front porch light on. If there were any other kids on the street, it was too dark to see them.

"Huh," his dad said. "It's not that late. Not sure why everyone's light would be off already."

But as they walked down the street, they noticed lights on inside the houses. In fact, they could see people sitting in their living rooms and watching TV from time to time - always motionless, never turning to see them, not even moving to take a drink or stretch their arms. Kevin started to want to go home again - but something told him that wouldn't make things better.

"You know, it looks like everyone closed up shop early this year," his dad said. "Let's hit that one house over there and head home."

Kevin looked ahead to the small home his dad was motioning towards - the smallest house on the street, and the only one with a light on that he saw. He'd never noticed it before, but they didn't spend a lot of time in this neighborhood outside of Halloween. It definitely stood out tonight.

The first thing he noticed when they got to the yard was the gnomes. There were a lot of them, in all shapes and sizes. Some looked like traditional little men in long white beards, others were fairies or cartoonish animals. One of them even looked like those giant statues of men's heads that were on that far-away island Kevin had learned about at school. That one looked different, though. Less colorful and more angular, it could have almost blended into the yard if he hadn't been looking closely enough.

"I bet this lady has cats," Kevin's dad said with a chuckle. Kevin looked up at him, confused. "You'll get it when you're older, bud." He paused and then said, "Old ladies have cats."

They walked the short, cracked concrete steps up to her house and banged on the door. A rustling sound could be heard inside, and then a crash - like an entire bookcase falling over.

"That didn't sound good…" Kevin's dad whispered.

The door flung open. It was an older lady, wrapped in a fuzzy pink robe. She adjusted her grey hair, pushing it out of her eyes.

"Oh, I'm sorry, I'd just about fallen asleep!"

"Sorry to bother you..." Kevin's dad started to say.

"The kids haven't been coming by tonight! Everyone must have been scared away by those awful people they've been talking about on the news…"

Kevin didn't know who she was talking about, but he was almost too distracted by her voice to pay attention to what she was saying. It sounded high like a woman's voice, but...almost too high. Like a man when he was faking a woman's voice.

"I know what you mean. Pretty much just us out here - there's a lot more people downtown, though," Kevin's dad said.

That's when Kevin noticed how tall the woman was. He thought of girls being shorter than boys, especially when they got older. Didn't all old people get smaller? But this woman was almost as tall as his dad. Maybe even taller.

She reached for an orange plastic bowl and bent down to meet Kevin's gaze. Even the way she bent seemed odd. Almost like she was bending more from the middle of her spine than her waist. He stepped back, knowing he shouldn't be rude, but feeling intensely uncomfortable.

"Oh, don't be scared, I have a nice treat for you," she said. She pulled a small plastic bag from the bowl with a folded piece of paper tied to it.

"Fresh, homemade cookies. You like cookies, don't you?"

Kevin nodded but didn't say anything.

"These are extra special, because they come with a surprise. When you eat them, open up this little note, and read it. You'll learn the most wonderful lesson. So many of the kids today don't learn any lessons at all, they're so focused on the TV set. But I don't watch the TV at all. And after you read this, I bet you won't either."

She looked Kevin in the eye and grinned. He expected her teeth to be old and stained, but they were immaculate.

"Thanks, miss," Kevin's dad said. "Let's go hit those other houses, bud."

The woman rose to her full height, the top of her head hidden by the door frame. She grinned at Kevin's dad and waved.

"Good luck. It's pretty quiet around here tonight."

Kevin and his dad both smiled and nodded, but they were moving pretty quickly toward the street. When they got there, the ground felt like it was starting to spin beneath their feet. They stopped, too confused to know which way was which for a second. Kevin's dad closed his eyes and took a deep breath. He held still for a second before opening his eyes back up and looking both ways to gather where his truck was.

"Let's just head home, bud."

As they walked, Kevin knew his dad was feeling what he felt. He looked up at him to make sure he was okay.

"Let me see those cookies she gave you."

Kevin reached into his bag and handed them to his dad. Usually, he loved chocolate chip cookies. But he couldn't think of a treat in his candy sack he was less excited to eat. His tummy turned at the thought of it.

His dad pulled the slip of paper from the cookies and read over it. He paused, trying to make sense of it, then he crumpled it up and pitched it into the woods.

"Religious freak…" he muttered.

Kevin wasn't sure what was on that slip of paper, but a creeping feeling started in his brain and made him wish he still had it with him.

Bad Dog

Amber Allen and her friend Megan were lost. They'd trick-or-treated in Walnut Parks a few times before, and they had friends that lived there. It shouldn't be a hard place to get around. But after walking down two streets since leaving Amber's mom's minivan, they couldn't figure out where they were to save their lives.

"Shouldn't we have already passed Katie's house?" Megan asked. She was dressed as Jem from the *Jem and the Holograms* cartoon, and her clunky plastic shoes were getting painful to walk in. If they weren't going to run into a single house that was actually giving out candy, she wanted to go home.

"I guess maybe we had to go up one more street first," Amber responded, even though she knew that didn't seem right. Her mom had dropped her off at Katie's house to play a hundred times, and she knew the route like the back of her hand. Where were they?

They should have stopped and turned around when they first got confused. Near the first intersection they ran into, a heavy wind whooshed by, twisting their hair in the air. They swore the world was spinning around them for a second.

When it was over, they were both standing trepidatiously, hands out and knees bent, trying to keep their balance.

"What was *that*?!" Megan shouted.

Amber paused, getting her bearings, holding on to her hat. She'd fought to go as Indiana Jones for Halloween, even when her mom tried to reason with her to at least go as Princess Leia. She got her way, but she would be in big trouble if she lost that hat. They'd had to borrow it from her uncle Jerry, and Amber's mom did not like talking to him.

"Maybe an earthquake?' Amber said, even though it sounded completely insane to her. Did they even get earthquakes around here? She'd never heard about one before.

They only had thirty minutes, though. That wasn't near enough time to hit all of Walnut Parks to begin with. They'd already lost time on a street where almost all of the porch lights were off, except for a weird old lady that gave them cookies. On top of all that, this was the first year Amber's mom had let them walk the neighborhood alone, and she'd made it very clear that they better be back to the van in thirty minutes. Otherwise, they might never get to trick-or-treat again.

The siren song of Skittles had convinced them to go down a couple more streets and see if the roads felt like they were shaking again. Now they weren't sure where they were anymore.

They walked toward the next intersection, hoping to find a house or a landmark that they knew. Unfortunately, what they saw instead was Eddie Albertson.

No one liked Eddie Albertson. He wore a long, dark trench coat that always smelled bad, and he called girls the worst names you could call them. He loved to brag about killing people's pets, even though everyone said it wasn't true. He was way older than the kids at the elementary school, but they seemed to be the only people he ever talked to. Amber wondered if that was because no one in his grade wanted to give him the time of day.

She wished there was another way around, but she didn't want to lose time going all the way back down a dark street when they were already lost to begin with. She tugged on Megan's sleeve to get her to move to the furthest side of the street possible, hoping Eddie wouldn't see them.

"Woof!" he shouted.

No luck.

Amber tried to ignore Eddie and pull Megan down the road opposite from him at the intersection, but Megan jerked away from her. She started walking towards Eddie.

"Are you lost, too?" Megan asked.

There was a moment of hesitation in Eddie's eyes, like maybe Megan called him on something that was very true. It didn't last long.

"Are you seriously stupid enough to get lost around here? This whole town is the size of a cat turd. Are you an idiot?"

Megan shrunk back. She thought with all the weird stuff going on, maybe they were all in it together. Amber knew better than that with a guy like Eddie.

"Stop being a jerk," Amber said, pulling on Megan's arm again, this time getting her to walk away from him.

She swallowed hard when Eddie started following them.

"Maybe you should stop being a dog," he said back. "You know what I do to dogs? You're the ugliest girl I've ever seen. I'd be doing you a favor…"

Amber looked at the whip that was part of her Indiana Jones costume. It was made from basic plastic, but when she'd whipped it across her bedroom, it had snapped her writing desk pretty good. She wondered if it would make Eddie back off if she tried to use it on him. Or if it would just make him madder.

Eddie flicked her ponytail.

"First, I'd cut off your tail…"

She didn't let him say anymore. She grabbed Megan's hand, and she ran toward the house closest to them, ignoring the driveway and cutting through the grass.

"What the…" Eddie got out, before he realized what was happening.

The yard that Amber and Megan ran into belonged to a three-story home that wrapped almost fifty yards across a circular driveway. Behind the house, they found a gentle slope that led to a creek surrounded by trees. They ran down the hill, Megan losing her plastic Jem shoes in the process, and they didn't stop until they got to the trees. Amber paused there, hiding behind a large oak near the water. She peeked out from around the side while Megan tried to catch her breath.

She saw Eddie come around the house slowly, looking in the windows of the house to make sure he wouldn't be seen. Then he went to the patio furniture that was sitting out on the house's back porch. He looked under their picnic table before giving up, kicking a plastic chair into the grass, and heading back to the street.

"What's wrong with that guy?" Megan cried.

"He's a psycho," Amber replied.

They waited for a second, Amber trying to decide how long before it was safe to head back to the street. Unfortunately, they had no idea where they were, and it wouldn't be hard to accidentally run into Eddie again.

"Maybe we should just walk by the stream for a minute," she posited.

"But I'll get my feet all muddy!" Megan yelled back.

"Shhh!" Amber responded, looking to see if Megan's shoes were still laying in the yard. Knowing a guy like Eddie, he would probably take them with him just to be mean.

"Let's just go," she said, shrugging a little.

They walked a little way down the creek, with Amber trying to remember if it ran by any of the houses that she knew around here. Nothing really came to mind. If they didn't run into some place she knew, they could always knock on the door of one of these houses and ask if she could call her dad. But in the time it would take him to drive to the park where her mom was, her mom would already be freaking out and wondering where they were. Plus, not many of these houses even seemed to have their lights on to begin with. It wasn't that late already, was it?

She heard something rustling in the woods.

"What was that?" Megan asked quickly, a sharp snap of fear in her voice.

"Probably just a deer," Amber thought, though she wasn't sure how much she believed it.

They continued to walk, but that rustling sound kept emerging from the woods just behind them - almost as if they were being followed.

"Shouldn't there be another road by now?" Megan asked. The thought had crossed Amber's mind. In a neighborhood with this many streets, it seemed like eventually they would have to run into an intersection. But it felt like they had just kept going on endlessly.

The noise from the woods behind them kept at a steady pace, never gathering speed or losing track of the girls. If it had been Eddie, it seemed like he would have done something by now. But who else would keep following them like this?

Amber took Megan behind a tree a few yards from the water.

"Wait here. I'm going to sneak back and try to see who that is. If it's someone safe, I'll ask them how to get help."

Megan's eyes grew wide.

"No! Don't leave me here!"

"It's okay. Stay here, and I'll be right back. Otherwise, we might be out here forever."

She walked a little further up from the creek, where the tree line met the backyards of the houses. She didn't see anyone behind them, so she walked slowly in the direction from which they had come, trying to focus on the darkness in the woods. Would she be able to see something eventually? Hopefully she could make out some movement in the dark before anyone saw her.

She stopped dead in her tracks.

It was huge. And it was looking at her.

It was the size of a bear - but it definitely wasn't a bear. Dark black fur and longer legs led up to a leaner, more muscular body, and its head looked like that of an overgrown wolf - skull wide, jaw long and filled with sharp teeth. Settled on its back haunches, it was over six feet tall. And then it stood up.

Amber was frozen. She wanted to run, but if she flinched, would it automatically be on her? There didn't seem to be any way she could outrun it. But she needed to tell Megan about it. She would be leading it right to her in the process, though.

She didn't remember starting to move. Suddenly, she was just going forward, hoping she didn't feel a terrible weight on top of her, smashing her into the ground, fangs digging into her back. She didn't risk a look back, but she could hear the gallop of feet and smell the noxious breath just behind her.

Who knows what would have happened if she hadn't tripped just as she got to Megan. But she did, sprawling across the ground, hat and whip flying off her costume. She turned and saw it starting to sniff Megan's hair, and she screamed.

"NO!"

It stopped. It turned to look at her. It took a step her way.

And then it sat down, back legs folded on the ground, front legs keeping its massive body held up in the air. It seemed to be panting.

Amber and Megan stood motionless in fear for a second. Then Megan squinted, thinking she saw something. She moved toward the massive beast.

"Don't..." Megan whispered.

But Amber was all the more sure of what she saw, especially as the monster twisted its head to the side to look at her.

"Wiley?"

At the sound of its name, the creature slid its front feet forward, laying down in a position that made it look like a big, furry sphinx. But Amber knew better.

It was her friend Katie's dog, Wiley.

"What are you doing?" Megan whispered, through gritted teeth. But Amber was lost in her own world as she walked forward and scratched Wiley behind his ears. He leaned his head over toward her, almost knocking her down in the process. Then he whined, and flopped over on his side.

Megan stared with her mouth agape, as Amber proceeded to walk around the other side of it and rub its belly.

"What is that?" she whispered, finally coming out from behind the tree.

"It's Katie's dog, Wiley," Amber said, the words flowing weirdly comfortably out of her mouth. This whole thing made sense to her somehow, but she wasn't sure why. If nothing else, she wasn't that scared anymore.

Megan walked forward and touched its fur. Wiley lifted his huge head suddenly, a stern look on his face. Megan toppled backwards, terrified. Then Wiley opened his mouth, panting again and seeming to smile in the process.

"What...what's going on?" she asked.

"I think we need to get home," was all Amber could say.

"Well, duh."

The two of them decided to make their way up to the road. Wiley's head turned, and he watched them go. He stayed resting on the grass, though.

"How could that be Katie's dog?" Megan asked. "Was there like a...nuclear leak?"

Wiley, as Amber and Megan had first known him, was a standard looking mutt - maybe some lab, maybe some terrier, maybe some Husky - dark grey and black in color. He didn't even come up to Katie's dad's knees, and he was especially gentle unless he felt threatened. The gentle aspect of him still seemed to be intact, but otherwise...whatever was happening in this neighborhood had definitely gotten to him, too.

"I don't think it works like that," Amber said, but she was silently searching for signs that she had begun growing at an abnormal rate herself.

"How would you know?!"

Amber sighed. Why Megan would want to start a fight right now of all times seemed ridiculous, but she did like to get her way. Sometimes they'd go weeks without going over to each other's house after Megan blew up at her. It usually ended with Amber's mom coming into her room and saying, "So, you haven't seen Megan in a bit..."

Fortunately, the coast was clear when they got to the road. Or as fortunate as that could be on a night when there should have been hundreds of other kids trick-or-treating in this neighborhood. At least there didn't seem to be anyone that would bother them.

"Let's walk down to the next street," Amber said. "If we don't know where we are at that point, we'll go to the first house we see with a light on and bang on the door until they let us in."

Megan thought for a moment like she might have a better plan. Amber stared back at her, unsure what else Megan might say. Did she want to go back and try to ride Wiley to safety?

"Fine," she finally said. "Let's just go."

They walked up to the road, noticing more and more homes had already gone completely dark - far earlier than most adults would go to bed. Amber tried to not think of that as a bad sign. Everything here was a bad sign, though. Nothing was normal. If she thought too much about it, she'd start crying and stop trying to figure out what to do next.

They passed a few houses on the way up to the intersection, but none of them seemed particularly familiar or promising. They wouldn't wait long after they turned the corner before going up to one of the next houses and knocking. Everything else was beginning to seem futile. Amber had to admit, though, something made her not actually want to go inside any of these houses tonight. She told herself if a man opened the door that she'd never seen, they would go to the next one.

As they walked, she thought about how her mom didn't want her to go as Indiana Jones. The more she thought about it, the more she thought she made a pretty good Indiana Jones.

"Hey!"

The voice ripped into the quiet night, and Amber's heart was beating hard as soon as she heard it. They were in the middle of the intersection, and every house immediately felt very far away.

Eddie started stalking up to them, taking something from his pocket.

"Did you think that was funny?!" he yelled.

Megan was crying, and when Amber pulled on her this time, she didn't budge. She was welded to that spot in fear.

"Help!" Amber shouted.

"Shut up!" Eddie yelled. "There's nobody here! Everyone's gone! Do you see anyone?!"

Amber ran at him, barreling into his stomach and trying to knock him over. She hit him as hard as she could in the stomach, and it knocked him back. But it didn't knock him down.

He grabbed her by the ponytail and pulled hard. She screamed.

"SHUT UP!" he yelled again.

She wasn't sure what to do. She wasn't sure what else she could do.

A deep growl came from the darkness beyond the trees.

It was so loud, so harsh, that it managed to take all three of them off guard, even in the midst of the violent chaos Eddie was causing.

He let go of Amber's hair. He walked toward the sound, swinging the object from his pocket outward. He flicked open a small switchblade. A gasp caught in Amber's throat, horrified to think what he might do with it.

She might have felt better if she could have seen the look on Eddie's face, eyes wide, shaking, sweat suddenly dripping from all over him. He took each step like his feet weighed as much as bricks, body drawn toward a sound that his mind seemed all too aware he should run away from.

Wiley pounced.

He'd been much closer than any of them had realized, dark fur blending in with the night. He managed to clear the space between the two houses on the corner and the street in a single bound, teeth sinking into Eddie's back and chest as he did.

Tomorrow, both Amber and Megan will wish they had looked away. They will spend a lifetime wishing they had covered their ears. Anything other than watch what Wiley did to Eddie as he shook him back and forth, anything other than hear the sounds Eddie made while he did it.

At least Wiley didn't finish him there. With Eddie barely able to resist at that point, Wiley pulled him back into the depths of the woods.

The girls shook in place. Amber looked down to realize that, at some point, Megan had grabbed her hand and was still holding it tightly. She tried to stop herself from shaking, but her body wouldn't let her. It wasn't done processing what it had just experienced. It wouldn't be for a very long time.

Even with all the insane events of the night, the girls had never felt more lost than right then. Where could they even go, as each street seemed to change, as each house seemed unfamiliar, as each step forward in any direction just seemed to cement the fact that they were nowhere they knew anymore.

And then Wiley emerged from the woods.

Except he wasn't the same version of Wiley from the creek. Now he was just Wiley, as Amber and Megan had seen him a hundred times before. A squat little dog, not as tall as either of them. The only difference was that his fur seemed a little...damp.

He walked up to Amber and pressed his head against her leg, looking for attention. He left a red smear across her pants, but she steeled herself and scratched behind his ears anyway. The last thing she wanted was for him to lose his calm. He seemed genuinely happy to have her next to him, shoving the back of his neck up against her hand and rubbing it back and forth.

Amber looked to Megan, who was staring, mouth still open, small tears in her eyes. Amber reached out to her and patted her on the shoulder, much like how she had patted Wiley.

"I think it's going to be okay," she said.

Wiley started to walk away from them, but halfway down the street, he paused. He looked back at the girls, tail wagging. When they didn't follow, he walked back to them and whined. He started down the street again, stopped, and looked back at them once more.

"I… I think he wants us to follow him," Amber said.

Megan looked at her like she'd just started radiating bright green.

"I mean, he did protect us?" was the best Amber could muster. "Maybe he wants to take us back to Katie's house?"

She knew it sounded absurd, but what else did she have to go on?

The two of them started to follow Wiley, as he trotted happily down the street. He never stopped panting, tail wagging back and forth.

On their way back, Amber still struggled to recognize the houses. She caught sight of the one little home where they'd actually been able to trick-or-treat, surrounded by garden gnomes, and she swore she saw the old woman watching them from the window. But she wasn't going to stop now. Wiley was leading them somewhere, and she hoped it would be someplace safe.

And then he was gone.

She didn't see when he disappeared. It was more like she blinked, and Wiley failed to be there when she opened her eyes. She ran forward, worried they'd lost him, that this nightmare was about to start all over.

At the end of the road sat the park from which they had left, and parked right next to it was her mother's minivan. She almost fell over in disbelief when she saw it, but sure enough, there was her mother in the driver's seat.

She and Megan approached the door to the van warily, wondering if Amber's mother might be some kind of bizarre creature in her own way now. When they opened the door, though, she sat there normal as ever, reading her romance novel, drinking some tea. She barely looked like she'd skipped a beat while they were gone.

"Back already?" she said as they climbed in.

"Huh?" Amber said.

"Oh, I figured you'd be running up to the car twenty minutes late. Did you even get to the end of the street?" her mom asked.

Amber was at a loss. She had no idea what to say. She looked at Megan for a response, but she was just staring at the floorboards of the car.

"Oh, did you girls get in a fight again?" her mom asked.

There was a deathly silence. Amber had no idea what to say anymore. It should be a simple question, but she just wanted to scream. That didn't even seem like enough, though.

"No…" Megan finally murmured. She reached out and held Amber's hand and looked at her for a second. She didn't say anything else, though.

"Well, that's good. I guess if you're petered out, we'll go ahead and get you home. You'll be able to get a good night's sleep that way."

As her mom pulled the minivan on the street, Amber looked down at her pant leg. It was still smeared red. She squeezed Megan's hand a little harder. She definitely wasn't going to get a good night's sleep tonight.

October 31, 1985, Part 5

There were still a couple of kids milling around Kevin's neighborhood when his dad pulled the truck up to their house. Kevin usually didn't bother much trick-or-treating there himself; the houses were few and far between, and there were a lot of adults that didn't participate anyway. There were a couple houses they could potentially hit, though.

"Want to go to a few more before bedtime, bud?" his dad asked.

Kevin honestly didn't want to. He just wanted this whole freakish night to be over. But he also found himself not wanting to go inside their home, either. The closer they got to their front door, the more anxious it made him feel.

He nodded to his dad.

"Yeah, we can do a couple more."

They started at the house to their right, the opposite direction from the Jacobs house. They knew their neighbors there, the Caldwells. It was an older couple who had always been friendly to Kevin. When they opened the door, Mrs. Caldwell looked as sweet as ever, dressed in a long black shirt with a grinning pumpkin on it.

"Oh, look who it is!" she shouted gleefully. "Edgar, come look who it is!"

Mrs. Caldwell looked behind her, but there wasn't even a hint of movement or sound. She waited what seemed to Kevin like an oddly long time for a response.

"I haven't been able to get him away from the TV all night," she said. She finally shook her head, and turned back to Kevin with the same big orange candy bowl he'd seen all over the place tonight.

"We've got York Patties, and we've got Twizzlers. Which one do you want?"

"Ummm…"

"Oh!" she shouted, "I'm just kidding! You get both of them, of course, of course. All of the neighborhood kids get both of them." She picked one of each up and dropped them in his bag. The fact that just a couple pieces could make the plastic rattle the way it did reminded Kevin that he'd only gotten so much candy tonight. The whole night was off.

"And who do we have here?" Mrs. Caldwell asked. Kevin turned to see another kid about his age walking up the drive. It was James Gnarr, a boy just above Kevin's grade.

"Hey…" Kevin said, half waving. James nodded back to him, but he didn't say anything. He always seemed like a quiet kid to Kevin. It surprised him, because Kevin always felt like bigger kids could do or say whatever they wanted. Who was going to stop them? James was the kind of kid that made Kevin's dad say, "He's gonna be a linebacker!"

James silently held up his bag to Mrs. Caldwell as Kevin and his dad started to walk away. Kevin thought he heard him mutter a "Happy Halloween" before Mrs. Caldwell exclaimed, "Well, what are *you* supposed to be?!" Kevin never heard James respond.

As they walked away and lost sight of James, Kevin realized he didn't quite know what James was supposed to be, either. Was he even wearing a costume? And why was he being so surly? It really did seem like this Halloween was being rough on everyone for some reason.

Kevin and his dad moved to the next house, and the next, and the next. They never saw James again somehow, which would usually have seemed odd, as they went around the whole loop that was Maple Street. But Kevin was too driven to notice. He found himself wanting to push ever forward, get more candy, leave no door in the whole neighborhood without knocking on it. Unlike in Walnut Parks, the houses around Kevin's home were wide awake. He wanted to hit them all.

As they finished the loop that took them down the main drive into the neighborhood, they could have taken a right turn back toward their own home. That would have taken them past the Jacobs house, and Kevin knew his dad didn't want to go there. He turned left instead, taking Maple Street downhill into a part of the neighborhood where they rarely went. A few lights had started to go out, but for the most part, Kevin was still getting candy at each house he went up to.

His dad didn't start to get frustrated until Kevin had scoured all the nearby side streets, taken them down to where Highway 18 intersected with Maple, and started to head down the highway to the homes a few blocks away.

"Hey bud, where are you going?"

"There's a sidewalk," Kevin said bluntly. "It's safe to walk down it."

Just as he said it, a re-built pickup truck on comically huge wheels flew down the highway, revving its engine loudly. Kevin winced at the timing.

"Yeah, I know there's a sidewalk," his dad said. "But it's getting way too late. There's no reason to walk all the way down there. You've got enough candy."

Kevin stood completely still, staring back at his dad. He didn't want to go home. He couldn't go home.

"Bud, we've had a nice night," his dad said. Kevin bit the inside of his lip. That was a lie. "Don't make a fuss now. Let's just go home and eat some candy and watch some TV."

Kevin winced at "watch some TV." That was the last thing he wanted to do.

His dad crossed his arms. Kevin stared back. He ran through the options in his mind. He could go home, or he could run away. But he'd played the "run away from home" game when he was a little kid. There was only so far you could go. Eventually you had to go back.

Resigned, he started walking toward his father - and home.

"That's a good boy," his dad said. "Let's see what's on the TV…"

Sugar Sweats

James Gnarr was supposed to be a pirate. He didn't really care what he was, though. He'd put on the dark vest over a white, long-sleeve shirt, he'd put on the patch, he'd put on the big hat and the hook hand. But all he wanted was the candy. And as he'd walked, the cheap, flimsy hat had kept wanting to blow away, so he'd taken it off. The eye patch rubbed his face and made it feel like he was getting a rash, so he threw it in someone's trash can. And he got tired of holding the hook, so he dropped it in the candy bag. To most people, he probably just looked like a kid in a vest now - as likely to be a matador or a gangster as anything else.

But he hadn't really wanted to be a pirate to begin with. He wanted to be some kind of superhero - maybe Spiderman or Batman or the Hulk. His parents said no one was going as superheroes this year, though, and that he'd look like a dork if he did.

He sure didn't feel very cool dressed as a pirate.

That's part of the reason he'd talked his parents into trick-or-treating alone this year. They would drive him to each new neighborhood, but he would get to walk house to house by himself. He'd told them it was because he was too old to have his parents with him at every house, and that he'd look like a baby if they were there. It was more so that he couldn't stand them.

James' parents couldn't get on the same page - with him, each other, or anyone else. The things they could find to fight about sometimes boggled the mind, even arguing about which parking spaces they thought were the closest to the front door at the grocery store.

Sometimes James thought they started arguments with him just so they didn't have to argue with each other for a while. He could be eating a bag of Doritos, and one of them would suddenly freak out about how many chips he'd had that day, and if he'd had any vegetables, and if he'd had enough exercise.

That's why he wanted to trick-or-treat alone this year. He could go where he wanted, eat candy as he walked, not have to worry about if he was doing something wrong and about to be yelled at. No chance that his parents would get in an argument with each other at some random house, and James would have to stand there awkwardly, getting sympathetic eyes from someone who wouldn't even give him a little extra candy as a "sorry, kid."

That said, he was finished up on Maple Street and had to head back to the car. He wished he could go somewhere else, but the only way home was through his parents.

But once he got there, he could eat his Squirmy Bar.

"If you needed to get some more work done, you just could have stayed home!" he heard his mom shouting at his dad when he got in the car.

"I didn't say that!" his dad fired back. "I just said that I needed to run some numbers as soon as we got home!"

For the first part of the drive home, they were too busy fighting to say anything to James. Then his dad noticed him eating a Milkshake bar.

"How much candy have you had tonight, James?" his dad asked.

"Like...two pieces," James shot back.

"Oh, I definitely think it's been more than that. You've had another piece every time we've gotten into this car, and you've been in and out at least five times. When we get home, the bag of candy is going up in the pantry. You can have two pieces a day, but you need to start losing some weight, son."

James bit hard on his cheek. He was trying not to snap back at his father. He knew he would just get in more trouble if he did.

"Did you hear me? Say something, son."

"Yes, I heard you!" James shouted, his resentment leaking through.

"Don't get an attitude with me! We can throw that whole bag of candy out!"

"Would you leave him alone, John!" James' mom countered.

"If he doesn't learn now, he never will! There's been too much of this stuff lately…"

Another fight was brewing. James should have known his dad would find a way to ruin Halloween, but they'd come so close. He tried to block it out by thinking about anything else. He started going through the different types of candy in his bag - Nerds, Milky Way, Butterfinger, Lifesavers, Mounds, the Squirmy Bar - and when he would eat each one. Then he tried to think about what the best costumes he'd seen were - that Stay-Puft Marshmallow Man, Inspector Gadget, the wolfman who looked so much like an actual wolfman that he'd done a double take. He thought about some of the best decorations he'd seen - a jack-o-lantern carved like Woodchuck from Charlie Brown, the giant spider hanging from Mrs. Willoughby's door, the house over by Sparrow's Creek that turned its front yard into a full-on cemetery, with one tombstone even named after the president. But no matter how much Halloween he tried to conjure up in his head, it couldn't drown out his dad's complaining.

When they got home, James was careful not to take any more candy out of his bag - and to even try to hide it behind himself a little - until he got to his room. In his experience, even when his dad made a big announcement of a punishment or threat, he usually forgot it five minutes later. He'd gotten off on a rant about taxes before they got to the house, and it was the perfect distraction for James to get his candy bag to his bedroom.

The first thing he did was pick out the Squirmy Bar.

New candy was one of James' favorite things in the world. Any new combination of chocolate, nougat, wafers, fudge - anything but peanuts. Gummies, sour stuff, candy corn, taffy - those were all good. But a new chocolate bar that wasn't just a rehashed Three Musketeers? That was always something to be excited about.

He couldn't believe it when the old woman had dropped it in his bag over in Walnut Parks. They'd gone out extra early, because James' dad had made a big deal about how he didn't want to be out very late. Even with how quickly it seemed to get dark tonight, they were out of Walnut Parks before the sun went down. It had been a good haul, with lots of adults bringing out the big guns - letting you take handfuls of candy from their bowls, mixing up multiple types of candy to give you a good spread, and the ultimate - handing out full-size candy bars. And one he'd never heard of to boot? James had almost wanted to skip the creepy house surrounded by gnomes; now he would always be glad he didn't.

The Squirmy Bar wrapper didn't say exactly what was in it. It was bright purple with the words "Squirmy Bar" spelled out by what looked like a giant, rainbow-colored worm. It's eyes sat at the top of the "S," a little tail hanging off the bottom of the "r." What was most fascinating about it, though, was as you turned the package around, it almost seemed like the shape of the candy bar inside moved into different configurations.

He paused for a moment, though, when he turned the package, and it was almost like he saw the candy bar shift around rapidly - like something trying to wriggle out of his hands.

How did they pull that off?

"James, get out here!"

His dad's voice was loud and had an edge to it. Something had gone wrong. He started to stand up when he heard the kicker.

"And bring your candy!"

He knew where this was going, and his face became flush with anger. He grabbed the candy bag off the ground and prepared to surrender it to his dad for the night. He paused, though, throwing a couple of small pieces and the Squirmy Bar under his bed.

He muddled slowly into the living room, greeted by his dad's sour face and his mom already reading her Stephen King novel. He stood there, silent, waiting for the inevitable tongue lashing.

"Well?" his dad said.

James didn't respond. He wasn't sure what he could say to defuse the situation.

"Didn't I tell you to give me that candy when we came into the house? And did you?" Before James could respond, his dad added, "You went in the bedroom and ate half the bag."

"No, I didn't!" James might be willing to cop to what he did, but he definitely wasn't going to get in trouble for what he didn't do.

"I don't believe that for a second! There's about to be some real changes around here, young man. Don't think Santa's coming down that chimney if you don't get your rear in gear for the next couple months."

There is no Santa, you stupid old fart, James thought to himself. He looked to his mom for help, but her face wasn't coming out of that book for anything. James was on his own in an unwinnable situation. He decided to turn around and just head back to his room, hoping his dad would let him be.

"Hey! Did I say we were done?"

If James had bit the inside of his lip any harder, his teeth would have gone right through it.

"Get up early tomorrow. We're doing push-ups and sit-ups before you go to school. And we're going on a run. Now give your mother a hug before you go to bed."

James' mom lifted her head, confused at first, then slightly irritated, and finally seeming to decide she needed to show James at least a little affection after his dad's onslaught. She hugged him tight and whispered, "Get a good night's sleep. You've got school in the morning."

The news was on as James headed back to bed. He heard the news anchor say something about devil worship as he walked into the hall. That usually would have sounded interesting to him, but at that point, all Halloween fun was pretty much shot.

All he had left was the Squirmy Bar. Before he ate it, he pulled off his silly pirate costume, getting as comfy as possible in his Superman pajamas. He crawled into bed and carefully pulled the Squirmy Bar wrapper open along its back seam. He didn't care if he got chocolate crumbs everywhere, but he was worried it would be melted.

To his pleasant surprise, it wasn't melted or broken up or anything. In fact, the bar curved around in a perfect, shallow S-shape. Usually, candy bars with funny shapes were sure to break apart before he ever got the chance to open them. He thought about just how often he'd lost the delicious chocolate ridges in Reese's Peanut Butter Cups to the jagged black wrapper around it. Somehow, the Squirmy Bar remained pristine.

He lifted it to his lips, slowly bit into the soft chocolate covering, and Heaven exploded in his mouth.

Cherry Mash, Mallo Cups, Cream Drops - James thought he'd tried it all. The Squirmy Bar tasted like nothing quite else that he'd ever had. The inside felt gummy - dark cherry flavored. He'd had chocolate covered gummies before, though, and the tastes never quite worked together. Something about this was different. The gummy wasn't so rubbery that you couldn't bite right through it, but it wasn't so soft as to feel like cream or nougat. It smooshed between his teeth almost like - a piece of steak? The comparison seemed bizarre because the inside of the candy didn't taste like meat, did it? It was almost like the inside of a cherry sour, but less sour and more...smoky.

James set the candy bar on the little desk next to his bed and tried to contemplate what he was eating. The texture didn't add up. He picked it back up and stared closely at the red material, trying to make sense of it. It was shiny and slick, but as close as he looked, he couldn't see the little bits of sugar crystals he usually associated with the inside of sour balls. But then again, it wasn't the exact kind of gel you saw in a standard gummy.

You couldn't actually put meat in a candy bar, could you?

He took another bite, determined to figure out what it was.

The second bite was just as good as the first, and he savored each chew of the exquisite concoction. He moved his tongue around to spread out the flavor as much as possible. He'd never been so curious or excited by a new candy.

And then he did something he never would have expected of himself; he sat the Squirmy Bar back down and decided to save the rest of it for later. Rare was the time that James wouldn't plow through something that tasted so good like he hadn't eaten anything in months. This might have been the first time he ever felt like he just *had* to share something with his future self, even if that made him painfully jealous of tomorrow's version of him.

As he drifted off to bed, the temperature in the room was just right. A little cool, just enough to make his pillow comfortable. He liked it to be chilly enough that he wanted to pull up the covers to keep warm. Fortunately, his dad kept it cool in the fall and winter, always shouting about how, "It's not gonna hurt anyone to put on a sweater!"

It was much warmer when he woke up. Every once in a while, James would fall asleep with his socks on, and he would wake up on fire, covered in sweat. This felt like those times, but he wasn't sure why it was happening. He kicked the heavy sheet off him and laid there for a bit, but it didn't actually cool him down.

Then his stomach started to gurgle.

There were few things James hated more than when his tummy acted up after eating too much candy. Following a particularly indulgent trip to the skating rink one night, he'd realized Twizzlers, Peanut Butter Cups, and Pepsi were a particularly dangerous combination for that kind of reaction. When all in the world he wanted was some sleep, he'd been on the toilet, trying hard to expel the aftermath of his snacking. His stomach even tricked him into thinking everything was okay again after letting out some gas, but ten minutes later, he was right back in the bathroom. He didn't get back to sleep until after 3 am that night.

He crept down the dark hall to the bathroom, hoping tonight wouldn't be as bad. He tried to make sure he didn't wake his parents as he went. If they knew he'd been up late to go to the bathroom for an hour, his dad would definitely rub it in his face in the morning.

Catching just the slightest glimpse of himself in the bathroom mirror, he thought his face might have looked a little rounder tonight, but he shook it off. It was late; he was tired. He needed to send these candy bars to their grave and be on his way.

As soon as he sat down, though, it was obvious that wasn't going to happen.

All of James' distress remained in the upper part of his gut, squishing and groaning but never dropping down toward his bowels. Also, it seemed to be...moving. He'd had gas before, the shaking and rumbling of his guts as it tried to shift to new spaces and find a way out. Eventually, it always did.

But this was different. It still felt solid and slimy inside him, like an eel was swimming around inside his belly, almost up to his chest. No matter how much he tried to open up his lower intestine and push it out, it stayed there, at times feeling like it was even trying to move toward his throat. James shook it off and continued to push, but this type of ordeal had never felt so helpless.

After fifteen minutes or so, he gave up, pulling up his pants and heading to the sink to wash his hands. That's when he first saw it. The thickening of the bottom of his neck, almost like an extra layer of flesh had been wrapped around it. If he stood up completely straight, it almost went away. But when he slouched and bent over to run the sink, it was very, very apparent. He wondered if he could have put on some weight with just the candy he ate tonight, but this was unlike anything he'd ever seen.

"Dang it," was all he muttered, though, drying his hands and heading back to bed. A few years down the road, he might have been alarmed as he should have been. Tonight, though, he just didn't want to get in trouble. He slid back under the covers, but immediately kicked them off again to cool down.

He took another bite of the Squirmy Bar to make himself feel better.

It's hard to say if James ever fell back to sleep or if he just felt everything that happened and told himself it must be a dream. He felt the space between his fingers fill up with a combination of bloat and moisture. He couldn't be sure when he no longer felt the difference between each of the individual digits, but it was probably near the time he realized he could no longer lift his head and look down - his neck and shoulders and head merging into one shape, thick white rings on top of rings, leading up to a puckered hole for a mouth, two dark eyes floating near the top of his head. He wasn't aware of all the goo now dripping from the translucent skin of his body, but he could feel a mucus deep in his throat, burning and soothing him at the same time.

He went to stand up, only to find his legs had merged into the same tubular, viscous mess as the rest of his body. Trying to look down, he struggled to lift what was once his head, but instead the force propelled his eyes floating down the length of his new, maggot-like body. As they drifted, he noticed his clothes hadn't been pushed off by his transformation, but instead, absorbed inside of his body. They seemed to be slowly decomposing, little holes forming at the edges of them.

Neither of his eyes finished moving until they reached the other end of his new form. As they settled near the end of the bed where his feet should be, he found a new mouth now generating at this end of his body, opening up in an O-shape that sucked in air, but quickly shut on its own accord when it didn't take in any delightful sugars.

This was going to be difficult to explain to his parents.

By some force James was yet to understand, he sent his eyes back up toward the other end of his body, near the headboard of the bed. He tried rolling his head to the side, near the desk that sat next to him; it worked. He opened the mouth at this end of his body, and he sucked in what was left of the Squirmy Bar.

The sweet sugars hit him like a shock to the system, and the rest of the gummy sludge at the center of the Squirmy Bar flowed throughout him, expanding his skin and letting loose a new splurge of mucus that helped him to slide his body around. He worked his way off the bed, on the floor, and tried to decide what to do next.

The obvious choice was to go to his parents' room and tell them he'd turned into some sort of slug creature and needed help. He couldn't imagine how much trouble he'd get into for *that*. If he couldn't eat a few candy bars on Halloween without getting chewed out, who knew how his dad would punish him for turning into an invertebrate and dissolving his favorite pair of pajamas inside himself. If nothing else, he would definitely take away James' Halloween candy.

He decided to finish it all off before his dad even got that chance. Fortunately, he'd left his bedroom door open ajar so he could squeeze out of it and down the hallway to the kitchen.

It was almost insulting how many places there were to hide candy in their house, yet James' parents always put it at the top of the same cabinet drawer. It was like a test. Would he just pull up a chair and climb up on the counter to steal it back, knowing he would get in more trouble if they noticed any of it was missing? Or would he just pretend he didn't know it was there, giving them the satisfaction of thinking their hiding place was far better than it was?

Right now, James didn't care. Instead, he smushed his body against the wall next to the kitchen cabinet, sticking to it and inching his way upward a flesh ring at a time toward the candy bag. Once he reached the ceiling, he leaned himself toward the cabinet, opening his mouth hole, sucking in wind, delighting as he pulled the bag directly into himself. There was no unnecessary unwrapping candy, chewing it, licking his fingers. Instead, he felt it start to melt away all throughout him, like his body was one giant tongue, delighting in the ultimate sugar rush.

"Did you hear something?" he heard his dad mumble to his mom down the hall. James froze in place, wondering what to do next. Could he get back to his room before his dad came out? Could he even close the door if he did?

He started milling through various excuses he could give his parents, not understanding the idea that he could no longer talk. He couldn't think of much. He was going to get swatted, hard, maybe even with a belt.

On another night, he might have been doomed. But hanging down from the wall, he noticed something. Underneath the cabinets was the kitchen sink, and just in front of the sink was the kitchen window. From time to time, James' mom would open it up and throw scraps out for whatever critters happened by. But last time she did, she'd left a small space between the bottom of the window and the window ledge. James seemed far too big to squeeze through that crack, but some guiding impulse led him down that way.

It wasn't a comfortable fit. There wasn't much left of James' body that was totally solid, but his eyes and some of the debris floating inside himself were solid enough that they squeaked and shuttered as he tried to squish himself out the window. But he found his body flattening and twisting and contorting until he was almost dripping out of that crack under the window into the backyard. He wriggled out with most of the candy still intact, though he felt the end of his pajamas bunching up on the window frame and finally popping from the mouth on the back side of himself. What was left of them lay soaked in slime in the sink.

James would never know, though. He was wriggling through the backyard, trying to figure out where to go next. Logic told him to go to a hospital or find an adult that wouldn't yell at him, but the depth of his inner drive just kept saying, "...sugar."

But where would he find sugar? Everyone had gone to bed for the night, and he wasn't sure he would receive the best response if he tried to slither into the store or anyone's home like this. Why had sugar been so easy to get a few hours earlier but was now so difficult to...sugar.

What happened next wasn't something James actively thought through in detail. He simply moved. Squirming, inching, sliding along, driven by something he didn't understand, the entire idea of language and cognitive processing far from his experience of the world now. But somehow, he found himself at a house a block away, dragging himself on to a strangers' front porch, to an orange candy bowl they had left out at the end of the night. Milky Ways and Snickers. He wasn't sure how he'd known it was there, but he didn't care. He rolled back his circular lips and devoured the bowl of chocolate in front of him without a thought.

There came that familiar rush, glucose molecules radiating throughout him. He rolled in circles on the stranger's front lawn, gleeful, and then laid there for a moment. His senses started to go off again. *Sugar.*

In a perfect world, this could have gone on all night - James' imperceptible sugar sensors telling him to go this way and that. But at some point, he found himself in the middle of the city, with no real idea of how he got there. Whereas trying to move this way and that in his new body was difficult at first, he'd taken to it well now, rolling, wriggling, and squeezing into new spaces, along backyards, up in trees. Wherever the sugar in the air drove him, he found himself, one way or another.

But now he'd crawled over a fence from a residential neighborhood into a large string of businesses - a run of strip malls, just outside of the downtown area. He'd been led here by the local ice cream shop that was loaded with treats, but he was completely unaware there was no easy way inside its walls. He'd almost made his way to the front door, when a car came around the corner. Its headlights were blinding and painful to James, boring into his see-through skin and making him feel like he was actually burning. But the worst part was the car's passenger-side tire catching the back end of his body - what he might consider his "tail" since his eyes and mouth were currently floating at the other end. It smashed open his back side, shooting part of the goo and mucus from him and leaving tears in his ridged, roly poly skin. If he could have screamed, he would have. Instead, he just twisted and convulsed back and forth at the edge of the road.

In the sidewalk that lay in front of the ice cream shop was a sewer grate - slats of flat metal leading up to an empty access hole. It wasn't the biggest opening in the world, but if James could fit through the window in his parents' kitchen, he could squeeze through this. And that's just what he did, finding himself spilling down to the sewer walls under the ground, away from the dangers of the street.

There, it smelled...good. At least to James it did. If most people had found themselves in that part of the sewer, they would have gagged at the stench of leftover foods and the remnants of other people's waste. But all James could smell - on the walls, in the water, all around him - was the essence of the sugars from the ice cream shop just above him. Whatever had seeped down from inside that building had found its way here, to this dank spot somehow, and James was reveling in it.

He lost himself in that moment, crawling the walls, splashing in the water, finding ways to suck in the sweet scent all around him. He didn't need to go home. He didn't need to go anywhere else. This was the happiest he'd ever been.

October 31, 1985, 11:59 pm

Kevin had mainly stayed away from the television as he ate his candy that night, opting to pick out a piece and walk around snacking on it. He amused himself half by playing pretend and half by flipping through a book of Halloween games and facts he'd gotten at one of the local businesses. He varied the candy - some Runts here, some Hershey Kisses there, a small box of grape Nerds - never eating so many things at once as to set off his parents' health alarms. He snuck back to his bedroom to eat some of it, making sure they didn't see everything he ate. He put the empty wrappers in his backpack. When it came to gorging on Halloween candy, he was a pro.

The ritual of sucking down as much candy as possible had almost made him feel normal again. All of the weird things he'd noticed - that his dad had seemed all but oblivious to - were starting to fade from his mind. If you'd asked him about the weird old woman who had given him the cookies, he would barely remember who you were talking about.

Yet he couldn't stop feeling a nameless sense of unease. He hadn't touched those cookies. He was vaguely worried about that girl from school, Amber, but he wasn't sure why. And even though he would usually have tried to take the TV from his dad to watch Halloween cartoons, he had no interest in it tonight.

Maybe it was because he had some math homework he was putting off. But teachers never seemed to mind as much when you didn't turn in assignments the day after Halloween. They just sighed and said, "Of course."

Something caught his eye right before bed, though. His dad was watching an old black-and-white movie. James usually avoided black-and-white movies. He might watch some old episodes of *Dennis the Menace* or *Lassie* if he was restless and staying up too late. He'd tried watching some of the old monster movies like *Dracula* and the first *Godzilla*, but he couldn't do it. It wasn't that they weren't in color; they were flat-out boring.

This was different. He'd seen a creepy old man, gritting his teeth and chasing a girl in a graveyard. She'd gotten to her car, but he smashed the window with a rock and tried to pull her out. Even when she started driving the car downhill, she couldn't get away. James found his heart beating faster without ever realizing he was so engrossed in the movie.

His dad caught him watching right as she was running up to an old house in the woods. Night had fallen, and she was screaming.

"I think it might be time for bed, bud!" he said, popping out of his recliner and blocking the TV.

"But it's Halloween! I always get to stay up late on Halloween!"

"You did stay up late! It's after 10! And you've got school tomorrow!"

There was no use arguing, and Kevin wasn't the type of kid to argue anyway. He did as he was told, brushing his teeth and crawling into bed in his GI Joe pajamas.

No matter how hard he tried, though, he couldn't get to sleep. He closed his eyes, he flipped the pillow to get to the cool side, he tried counting sheep. He kicked the sheets off and put them back on. He even started telling himself a little story in his head about a boy who had almost the exact same day as he did - an old trick his grandma taught him before she died.

None of it worked. Not only that, every time he tried something, it felt completely stupid and pointless to him. Why even bother?

He looked at the clock on his bedroom desk. It read 11:30.

He wanted to know what happened to the girl in that movie.

Kevin had never crept out of bed at night, at least not since he was young enough to get so scared that he wanted to sleep with his parents. He wondered if it was the kind of thing he could get in actual trouble for, but some part of him didn't care. His brain itched, pulsed, begged to go back and see how that movie ended. What happened to the girl?

Every move Kevin made felt like a potential landmine. Even the rustle from peeling back the covers sounded deafening to him. A little piece of him told himself to stay in bed after that, but the loudest voice in his brain said, "No! We'll be quick! It's just down the hall!" His foot hitting the carpet, the twist of the door knob, the squeak of the hinges, his steps down the hallway - after each one, he stopped and strained his ears to hear movement from his parents' bedroom. But there was never even a peep.

The television presented the biggest trap of all. It had three knobs - a big one on top, right next to a tiny window that showed numbers for changing the channel; a similar one below it for adjusting the volume; and a small metal button below those two that looked like the cigarette lighter in his dad's truck. The first trick was obvious - twist the volume knob as far as it would go to the left to make sure the sound was already off before you ever turned on the TV. Kevin did this on occasion so his dad wouldn't know how long he'd been watching something, and he could pretend to be engrossed in a show that he'd just started watching.

The tricky one was the "on" button. When anyone pulled it out, the television flashed on with a bright light and a loud click, followed by a bass-y *"wuuubbb"* sound that filled up the room before quieting down over a couple seconds. Even with the volume off, this pattern was the same every time, and you just had to hope that no one noticed it. Kevin pulled the knob out as slowly and delicately as he could, but no amount of care would actually stop the initial light and sounds that popped out of the television set. He crossed his fingers that his parents snored right over it.

The flash of light seemed so bizarrely blinding that Kevin didn't even notice the sound, but what was weirder was what he saw on the television afterward. The black-and-white movie with the terrified girl running into the house in the woods was gone. Instead, the cartoon that was playing on the TV when he'd left for trick-or-treating was back on, even though it was almost midnight. Movies on the TV always went two hours; what had happened to the one that his dad was watching? And who puts a cartoon on at almost midnight?

Thinking his dad must have changed the channel before bed, Kevin started twisting the knob, flipping through channels to find the right one.

But the Halloween cartoon was on every single one of them.

Some of the channels did tend to show the same things; 3, 10, and 13 might have an episode of *Punky Brewster* on, while 2 and 7 would be showing a Disney movie. But Kevin had never seen the exact same show no matter how many times he turned the dial. He almost thought it was broken, but then he noticed how the image did indeed flicker each time he changed the channel, and how the image quality was a bit different on each channel - sometimes with a little static in the picture, sometimes with darker colors. But for whatever small differences existed, it was always the exact same show.

A dark grey castle filled the screen. It looked flat and two dimensional at first, just the outline of a shape with black lines running through it to create the look of bricks. As the camera moved toward it, though, the castle gained shape and depth, revealing itself to be made of stuffed cloth, like on a puppet show. But even on *Mr. Rogers*, it seemed like they showed a place that was fake and then another place that was real. This happened all at once, like the cartoon castle really did turn into the three-dimensional structure he saw now. How did they do that, Kevin wondered.

There were three bursts of static as the camera continued to move toward the castle. Each one revealed...a man in a skeleton mask? An actual skull that had human eyes and a dark background behind it? Kevin couldn't tell for sure, though it seemed like maybe the skull was...breathing. And its eyes were staring out of the TV. Why did it feel so much like they were looking at Kevin?

"Hey, Benny."

Kevin fell to his side and desperately tried to scoot away from the voice that had appeared next to his left ear. He looked in horror as the skeleton he'd seen from the cartoon now stood next to him. Its bones were animated like on the show, but they seemed to flicker, revealing what looked like a human body behind the image. Kevin turned to the screen to see if it was just some optical illusion, but what he saw made things worse: the camera diving into the door of the castle to dizzying effect, and the castle walls emerging from the TV itself, spreading around the living room.

"Benny!" the skeleton shouted. "We've got to get out of here! We're going to get trapped in the castle with...the Skull King!" Most everything he said matched the high-pitched voice the skeleton spoke with on the television show. But when he said "the Skull King," his voice sounded lower and cracked into a mechanical sound, like someone saying it over an intercom.

Behind the skeleton, Kevin could still see the window that looked out onto the Millers' front yard. His mom had hung a large plastic witch in front of it, and he could make out its silhouette. Even that flickered in the darkness, though.

And then it was gone.

Kevin searched the dark space around him, barely even aware of the curious skeleton still staring back at him. The air felt colder now, and he looked down to see a dusty concrete floor.

And he was...animated. A living cartoon. He was covered in blue-grey fur on the back, and a giant white stripe that ran down his stomach and the palms of his hands. Or were they paws? Feet? Something brushed him from behind, and he twisted his head in shock, only to find that he had a long, pink tail now. He was the cartoon mouse he'd seen on the TV earlier. His stomach turned hard at the thought.

"There's no one here," the skeleton said. It's voice had taken on an even higher tone. It had gone from sounding genuinely afraid to almost like it was mocking Kevin. Benny. No, Kevin, he thought to himself. *My name is Kevin.*

"We can't stop the Skull King if he's not here, Benny," the skeleton chided. "We need to get back across the moat before the drawbridge is raised. We don't want to get trapped here for forever...."

A terrible blast of noise tore through the darkness. It was like a giant viking horn blowing out the scream of an elephant. It lifted the dust off the ground around Kevin and the skeleton, and the wind blew Kevin's fur back. At the sound's screeching peak, everything around him blurred into grey static again. Through the static, he could vaguely see his home, his own human hands as they were only minutes ago, and in the place of the skeleton, the sight of a sad, frail old man with thinning hair. As the sound passed, though, the cartoon illusion returned.

"Uh oh, Benny, that's no good," the skeleton said. "We've got to go. I don't want to die."

Again, the skeleton's voice went flat and mechanical. Benny looked to meet his eyes. The skeleton wasn't moving now. It stared back at Kevin blankly.

Kevin started to walk past the skeleton, in a diagonal line that cut across their living room and took him to where their front door should be. Surely he would eventually bump into a wall if they were still in his parents' house. Maybe he could even find the door knob somehow, open the door, and run outside where this whole nightmare would be gone.

But no matter how far he walked through the space, he was never stopped by anything, no walls or door or furniture. Long after he walked the distance of the room itself, he found himself in the same old empty, dark space. And as he walked, the skeleton stayed still, only turning its eyes and then its skull to follow Benny.

"Where are you going, Benny?" the skeleton finally asked, its odd voice breaking the silence.

"My name's not Benny. It's Kevin," he responded.

"No, it's not," the skeleton said, a weird cheer in its voice. "It's Benny. And we're here to save Halloween from the Skull King." He said this last part with the kind of fake enthusiasm Kevin associated with adults who tried to trick children into enjoying things they knew they wouldn't otherwise.

"I want to go home…" Kevin stammered.

"I know, Benny! But I'm supposed to get my body back! And you're supposed to get all of the children's Halloween costumes so they can go trick-or-treating again!"

"What?" Benny asked.

"Don't you remember, Benny? You were running through the city, looking for Halloween candy on the ground. It's your favorite time of year! But then you realized there wasn't any, and the children were so sad everywhere you went. So you asked the horses on Main Street, and they said the children had woken up on Halloween morning and all of their costumes were gone. Their parents said the evil old Skull King that lived in the castle on the mountain had taken their costumes away in their sleep, and the children weren't allowed to go out without them, or the Skull King would see that they were children and trap them in his castle for forever. You said you were going to come up here and find all those costumes."

"But...but how did I meet you?"

"Don't you remember anything, silly? You found me crying in the alley. I'd gone to sleep in my costume because I was so excited for Halloween. And then when I woke up, my body was gone. You said you'd help me get my body back!"

"But you're an old man," Kevin said.

The skeleton didn't reply. It stared back at Benny, immobile, wordless, seemingly dead if it wasn't for its eyes. Kevin felt like one of them had said something that they shouldn't have. He shifted and looked around, uncomfortable, but the skeleton didn't respond to him. To Kevin...Benny...Kevin...

"I think we should find the drawbridge and get out of here then..." Kevin finally said.

"Good idea, Benny!" the skeleton shouted, suddenly full of fake joy again. "We sure don't want to get *trapped.*" Its voice went dead and mechanical again when it said "trapped."

They began walking through the darkness, Kevin trying to let the skeleton lead the way. Maybe if he could just get out of this room, this darkness, and get outside, maybe this would all fade away and everything would go back to normal. He didn't know what else to do. He looked down at his hands, hoping another burst of static might show him his human form. Even if it was only for a second, it would make him feel better. But the space around him remained solid, right up until they saw the soft light and heard water moving ahead of them.

Benny couldn't tell if they had rounded a corner or if the darkness had just been so thick that they couldn't make out the bridge until they were almost in front of it. But the crack of light turned out to be flowing in from the massive doorway, which wasn't a door at all. A giant open archway stood, blocked only by the drawbridge itself - drawn up to its highest position, parallel to the castle walls. A narrow walkway wrapped around the castle that Kevin could step out on, allowing him to scurry up the stone guardrail and peer down at the moat below.

What he saw made the world fall around him. The drop was far, but at the bottom was a faded blue color with small triangles moving through it, like he'd seen in cartoons hundreds of times before. The sound crashed like actual waves, but the water didn't look like it could hurt anything. If he jumped, would he die? Or wake up?

He felt something on his shoulder, and he twisted quickly.

The skeleton was just behind him, hand outstretched toward Kevin's back. It froze and said nothing. Was it trying to stop Benny? Or push him?

"I think we have to go back inside," Kevin said.

The skeleton said nothing.

"Don't you want to find your body?"

No response.

Suddenly, Benny wanted nothing to do with the skeleton or the water below them.

He started to back away. He made sure to never turn away from the skeleton, always keeping eye contact. As another blast of terrible sound and wind blew through the castle, static filled Kevin's vision again. The image of the skeleton danced back and forth with the image of the old man, now looking enraged and disgusted at Kevin. But even after the static stopped flashing, the skeleton never moved, watching Benny retreat from him while remaining dead still.

In the murky shadows of the castle, Kevin couldn't see much. But as he moved away from the light of the drawbridge, he saw a torch burning in the other direction. The closer he came to it, he saw it was part of a line of torches along the wall. They created just enough light for Benny to see the angle where the floor and wall met. There sat a trail of pumpkin seeds, leading the way forward.

Benny found himself struck with hunger. He crammed the first pumpkin seed in his mouth. He didn't chew it, though. He bent down on his front furry feet and walked to the next pumpkin seed, cramming it into his mouth as well. The whole process was making Kevin realize just how small he was now, just how much he was actually a mouse, but he couldn't stop to think about it. He just wanted more seeds. More, more, more.

One seed after another, he stuffed them in his mouth until he found himself in front of a massive door. There, he finally started to chew, crushing the seeds while he felt like he still had a chance. He wasn't sure what was behind this door, but he felt like it might be the last thing he would ever see.

A burst of static filled his vision. The door did not appear to be a door. It was an old gate, wood rotting, and behind it, he could see garbage and debris.

The horrible sound of elephant screams ripped through the air again, so close that Kevin thought his ears might bleed. As he covered them with his little feet, the giant door started to creep open, flashing back and forth in the static between being the decrepit gate and the door itself. When it finally came to a rest, only the imposing door remained.

Kevin wanted to run, but Benny grounded his feet. Where else can I go, part of him thought. Anywhere! Anywhere but here! the other half of him responded. That door, those sounds, nothing good could be in there! Yes, yes, but the only thing that can get us out of here might be in there as well.

He was frozen in place for a moment, Kevin and Benny clashing back and forth. Then he took one step toward the door. His tail wrapped around his stomach, and he held it there - a poor substitute for a shield, but the only thing that actually made him feel safe right now.

Inside the door was a grand room, lined with long, empty dining tables. They were dimly lit by chandeliers that hung high in the air, so high that Kevin couldn't fathom how tall the room was. Everything was coated in dust and grime, a dank, old smell permeating the air.

"I thought I told you to leave," a voice boomed from the opposite end of the room. It was painfully loud and seemed impossibly far away. Out of instinct, Benny dashed behind one of the filthy benches seated at each table.

"It doesn't matter where you hide. I can see you anywhere. Come down here and let's be done with it." The voice sounded a shade angry, but mainly weary and resigned. "I won't hurt you if you conduct yourself appropriately."

Shaking, Kevin stepped from behind the bench and started to walk down the center of the room. At the other end of it, he could barely make out a large platform that elevated another table in the air, a dark figure seated behind it. The simmering quiet of it all was unbearable.

"Hurry," the figure said. "We're running out of time."

Benny tried to push his tail back behind him. He wanted to look strong as he approached, but it kept trying to wrap back around himself in defense. Kevin hated moments like this - when your body gives you away, crying when you didn't want people to know you were sad, shaking when you didn't want people to know you're scared.

The figure behind the table rose, towering over Benny as he approached. He wore a long dark robe with a large hood. From the hood protruded a wicked set of antlers, twisting upward, left and right, at unpleasant angles and in jagged points. The figure pulled its hood back, revealing a head that looked like a massive deer skull, jaw full of graying teeth, half of them already decayed. As he was revealed, another ear-splitting scream tore through the room, and in the burst of static that appeared, Kevin saw the same face he'd seen earlier on the TV - a dark human skull, half cloaked, with a single eye peering out at him. As it flickered back to the deer skull, Kevin wasn't sure which face he found more disturbing.

"Why did you come here?" asked the Skull King, his voice sounding less like it was coming from his mouth and more as if it was deep inside his body.

Kevin wasn't sure what to say. He was just looking for a way back home. But Benny was looking for the Halloween costumes of the children in the local village. His mind swam as he tried to remember if he was Kevin or Benny, but he was having trouble telling the difference.

"You...took the children's costumes... They can't celebrate Halloween now. They're...they're so sad," he said.

The Skull King's mouth flew open with an earth-shattering scoff. Static flickered so hard across the room that as much as Kevin saw the Skull King's other form and the random debris around him, it also turned into pure darkness at times. Benny fell to the ground, shivering.

"Fool," the Skull Thing spat out sharply. "You think I took their disguises? Why?! This room, this whole castle was a tribute, an altar to All Hallows' Eve. Everything I did was for the children. We used to have such festivities here..."

Kevin didn't understand. Wasn't this the whole reason he was here?

"Then...then who?" Benny asked.

The Skull King let out another bitter, resigned laugh. He turned away from Benny, starting to pace the length of the platform.

"Who do you think left me up here? Turned my magic and my own home against me? Who accused me of being the Prince of Darkness, when they were so much more tools of his whims than I ever was?"

The massive antlers drifted downward as the Skull King shook his head back and forth.

"Who fastened me inside this body, to shame me, to vilify me, to make sure I never escape?" He drifted back into his chair and breathed deeply. "The children's elders. The very ones that gave them life."

Benny's small eyes grew wide as he leaned forward. He realized he was breathing harder. It couldn't be true.

"But why? Why would their parents do that?" Benny asked, eyes open wide.

The Skull King sat quiet. For a second, Kevin didn't know if there was anyone left inside of him at all.

"Because they did what people always do. They became aware of something. Of how time came upon them, of how the harsh winters ravaged their bodies, of how their days were numbered. So they created a ritual. And the ritual was to come here, to feast, to revel, to pay homage to the spirits around them. Some saw it as a way to ward off the horror of the world, some saw it as a last chance at joy before the horror took them to the grave. We had such times…

"But as people always do, they forgot why they carried out the ritual. So they practiced it less and less, and made it easier and easier on themselves. They turned to new spirits who said they had to sacrifice fewer things, they decided the children didn't need to feast, they said it was all the way of the past. And then they turned on me - the reminder of what they were, what they could have been if they had worshipped properly, and just how little they have become now.

"They took the children's costumes away to finally destroy our ritual. No more carrying on through the streets, no more communing with their neighbors and the ghosts of their ancestors, no more indulging in the decadence that makes them remember why they push through the cold, cold winter. And they will blame me. That way, the children will do more than fail the celebration. They will hate the very symbol of the ritual itself, a monster devoured by its own image, the children forever unaware of what they are even doing. Accidentally burying their history. Turning it into an unrealized offering to their new gods."

The Skull King grew quiet again. Benny looked from side to side. What should he do now? Where could he even go? What was the way forward?

"Sir…" he finally said to the great beast that sat before him. "Is…is there anything I can do to help?"

The great jaw of the King shifted back and forth.

"I do appreciate your company," he finally said. "Stay here with me tonight. In my great castle."

"But…but what about my family? Won't they get worried about me?"

"After what I have told you, what do you think of your family? Do you feel safe going back to them? Do you think you will be safe knowing what you know now?"

The silence afterward was deathly. Benny quivered in place. Suddenly, he was aware of not just what a very small mouse he was in this world, but what a small person Kevin was in his own.

"What…what will they do to me?"

"Who knows, but…" and with that, the Skull King motioned to his empty, decomposing castle. "We must only decide how much to trust people once we have seen what they hide."

From his cloak, The Skull King extended a long skeleton hand. Without knowing what he was doing, Benny scurried up the bony hand into the darkness of the billowing sleeve. He tried not to think about exactly what it was that he was crawling up as he moved around the crevices in the King's arm. When he reached the bottom of the hood, he crawled out of it and rested in the folds where the hood met the shoulders of the robe.

He suddenly felt very tired.

"Who...who was the skeleton I met when I got here?"

That let loose the first roar of laughter the Skull King had managed in several quiet minutes. There was no static this time, though.

Now Benny wasn't sure he wanted to know the answer.

"When the villagers first turned against me, they didn't think it was enough to leave me be and let memories of me fade. No, I had to be destroyed. That was the only way for their new way of life to be truly safe."

Benny's head nodded as his eyes started to droop with exhaustion. He was sleepy, but he continued to listen. It didn't seem fair for the villagers to treat the Skull King like that after all he'd done for them.

"They decided to send someone to desecrate my castle and do away with me. There was one proud young man eager to prove that he was no longer one of the children. He told the elders that he was strong, that he was smart, that he knew how to trick me. He dressed himself up in the bones of the dead, wrapping them against his skin with twine. He came to my archway and tried to tell me that he was an ally. That he was just like me. He was so sure of himself. But he was wrong..." the Skull King mused, with a sinister chuckle. "But he found out what it was to be like me. And now he will never leave these walls. He has been here for a very, very long time."

Benny shrunk down further, understanding the Skull King's magnificent power more and more. He felt a chill come over him.

"Do not feel bad for him, little mouse. If even a single one of the villagers ever came here to try and free him, I would let him go. But despite never hearing a single word from him, they assumed the worst. They abandoned him. And they never tried again, finally happy to let me fester here and try to forget me. People like that will not come together to help each other. They never do. The skeleton was just hoping to use your body in place of his own, a trade that would give him passage from the castle walls. You were smarter than that, though. You saw him for what he really was."

Benny turned in the crook of the robe, making a space to settle down. He tried to draw part of the cloth around him for more warmth. He was very, very tired, but he was also proud that he had done such a good thing.

"And I can sleep here tonight?" he asked.

"For tonight. But tomorrow, you will awake far from here, back home. But you will know. You will know what they all are. And you will have to decide what to do with that knowledge."

As Benny drifted off to sleep, he murmured, "But I'm safe for tonight?"

"Yes," the Skull King replied. "You are safe. As long as you are inside here with me, you are safe. Now close your eyes..."

And with that Kevin drifted off into darkness.

Epilogue: November 1, 1985

The first time Kevin awoke, it was to the feeling of someone grabbing him and shaking him. For a brief moment, his breath caught in terror. Then he gained his bearings as his eyes adjusted, making out the face of his father.

"Kevin! What are you doing out here?! Are you okay?!!"

He spoke somewhere between a shout and a whisper, voice urgent but worried about startling Kevin's mother at this hour.

"What...what time is it?"

"It's five in the morning," his dad said. "Why aren't you in bed?"

"I...was," was all Kevin could muster.

"No, I think you snuck out here to watch that movie I told you not to."

"No..." Kevin began, trailing off.

"You get up and get to bed. We'll talk about this in the morning."

Kevin was groggy, but he was able to take his dad's hand and get up off the floor. He stumbled to his bedroom, fell onto the sheets, and drifted off into a dark, dreamless sleep.

The second time he woke up, he wasn't sure if he was still dreaming - or if he was ever awake. He felt the hot sun creeping through the window on his face, but first thought it must be a blaze coming to engulf the earth. He felt the moisture from his sweat on his bed sheets and swore it must be some kind of slimy remnants of a terrible encounter. Even the sounds of his parents' morning routine sounded like the chaos of a battle gone awry.

But then his alarm went off - only a minute after Kevin found himself coming to. He squeezed his eyes shut before slowly opening them again, finding himself nowhere more remarkable than his own bedroom. It was 7:00; just enough time to eat some breakfast and be on the bus by 7:30.

He floated through his morning routine, nothing ever seeming quite real. Every word his parents said to him had to be repeated before he actually heard it. He forgot what he was doing in the middle of pouring cereal. His dad eventually caught him staring at the wall without a thought going through his head.

"I think maybe we need to get to bed a little earlier next year, huh, bud?"

The way he said it made it sound like he was implying something, but Kevin's mom didn't react at all. His dad must not have said anything to her about how he'd found Kevin passed out in front of the TV. That should have mattered to Kevin, but it barely registered with him. Nothing really mattered to him right now.

He usually would have caught the bus to school, but his mom offered to drop him off. She had to run some errands, and the school was on the way. Kevin just kind of nodded, not responding to something he would usually see as a treat. They could listen to the radio in the car, as opposed to listening to other kids on the bus scream for the whole twenty-minute ride to school.

As they drove out of the neighborhood, they saw a police car sitting in front of the Jacobs house.

"Oh, your father is always worried about that family getting into trouble. I wonder what happened."

Kevin didn't respond.

"Did you have a good Halloween?" his mom asked as Kevin leaned his head against the window.

"Yeah," was all he said back. She looked sideways at him, surprised.

"That's it? What was the best part?"

Kevin just shrugged.

"You need to talk to grown-ups when they talk to you, Kevin," she said, a note of condescension in her voice. "They know some pretty important things."

He bit back his desire to say something mean to her. Whatever grown-ups knew, he thought, they sure didn't like to actually let kids know much about it.

The kids at Kevin's school surged with energy. He felt like he was going in slow motion. Usually, everyone was tired the day after Halloween. It was like everyone else had dug into their candy to get a pre-class sugar rush.

Kevin wandered the playground for the few remaining minutes before class began. Everywhere he turned, though, he heard snippets of conversations he couldn't shake off.

"Did you hear what happened to James Gnarr?" he heard one girl say to another. "His cousin was telling my mom that they found him naked, in the sewer, eating candy he stole from other people's houses! And his leg was all messed up so he couldn't walk and they had to take him to the hospital! He won't talk to anyone!"

They sounded shocked, but for some reason, it didn't sound weird to Kevin. It made perfect sense, and he wasn't sure why.

He went over to the large dome that sat in the middle of the playground - the one built out of multiple triangles of steel bars - and he started to climb it. Usually the highest parts of it were reserved for the oldest kids, but Kevin found himself longing to get as high as he could, to get away from the ground. Nestling in one of the triangles near the dome's peak, he listened to the kids inside of it.

"No, they can't find her anywhere! They think Robbie must have done something to her, because his mom was her babysitter. But no one knows! The cops went over there and everything. They're hoping they find her soon."

They're not going to find her, thought Kevin.

The kids below Kevin kept talking, making fun of Robbie and his mom, completely unaware that Kevin was even there. He thought about dropping down and spooking them or telling them to shut up, but he was too tired to want to do anything at all.

The wind blew cold for a minute, and Kevin heard kids milling all around him. He decided to stay up at the top of that dome as long as he could. He hoped nothing would interrupt him.

"Kevin!"

The sound shot through the air like a football, and it felt like it hit Kevin deep in the stomach. He opened his eyes and looked down to see Charles Dunt, as awkward as ever, waving his hand up at him, then motioning for him to come down. It was almost time for class to begin, so he climbed bar by bar back to earth.

"Have you seen Boone?" Charles asked, more intense than he had ever sounded in his life.

For a second, Kevin couldn't remember anything. Then the events downtown all came rushing back. He suddenly realized they'd found Charles, but no one had ever been looking for Boone.

"No," was all Kevin said back.

"I haven't either. I..." Charles said, cutting himself off. "Something weird happened last night."

Kevin should have been curious, but he had a sinking feeling he knew where this was going.

"I'm not sure what it was, but every time I try to tell an adult, no one will believe me," Charles said. "But if you see Boone, tell me."

"What if I don't see him?" Kevin asked, with a stare that made him seem a million miles away.

Charles retracted a little, unable to understand why Kevin was acting the way he was. He turned and started to head back toward the school.

"I'll talk to you later, Kevin. School's starting."

School. That was the last place Kevin wanted to go. He wanted to run deep into the woods and not talk to anyone else today. Something told him that would just make things worse, though.

He trudged toward the side door to the school, watching the last few remaining kids head inside in front of him. One of the last ones was Amber. Seeing her gave him one of the few small jolts of happiness he'd felt all morning.

"Hey, Kevin," she said, sounding a little worn out herself. "Did you have a good night?'

"It was okay," he said. "Kind of...weird."

"I know what you mean. Sorry we didn't see you again in Walnut Parks. But we didn't see much of anyone."

She stopped talking, and Kevin felt the dead air linger between them. He knew what she meant, but it felt weird to bring it up. Like he would be making her go through a memory you wouldn't want to talk about again. He hated it when people did that to him.

"Well, I'm going to be late to class," she said. "I'll catch you later."

Kevin didn't know what had happened to her, but he knew it was something that had changed her. He could feel it in everyone he talked to, everyone he walked by, everyone he saw today. There were two kinds of people now. People that were still normal, and people who weren't anymore. He wasn't.

He was almost to his classroom when Michael Forrester came around the corner. The hallway was wide enough, but they stopped directly in each other's paths. The tardy bell rang; neither of them moved.

Michael wasn't wearing his baseball uniform today. It had been replaced by blue jeans and a black T-shirt. It was one of the most regular outfits that any kid could wear to school, but somehow it looked wrong on him. Kevin didn't know Michael well, but he had seen him around school, and he'd never seen him wearing anything like it. He wasn't certain about how he knew that, but he was sure of it.

In the back of his mind, Kevin heard the sound of elephant screams echoing. He tightened his muscles. Michael fixed him in the same icy stare he had yesterday. But today, Kevin met his gaze and didn't flinch. If other people had changed overnight, Michael was still exactly what he was when Kevin saw him in the office yesterday. Kevin had become something much different, though.

Michael moved first, giving Kevin a wide berth on his way to class.

When Kevin got to his classroom, Mrs. Mellon said something to him, but he didn't hear it. He continued walking back to his desk, took his seat, and stared straight ahead. All of his teacher's words would fall on deaf ears today. Kevin wasn't thinking about anything else. He was only waiting for Halloween next year.

He would be ready.

About the Author

Joshua Coonrod grew up in Rolla, Missouri, watching *Godzilla* movies, pretending to be The Flash, and eating Junior Mints by the pound. He went to the University of Missouri and the University of Florida before receiving a PhD in Communication & Culture at Indiana University in 2018. He currently lives in Louisville, Kentucky.